THEREFORE I AM

Digital Science Fiction Anthology 2

DIGITAL
SCIENCE
FICTION

THEREFORE I AM
Digital Science Fiction Anthology 2

Published by: Digital Science Fiction, a division of Gseb Marketing Inc.
1560 Argus Street, LaSalle, Ontario, Canada—N9J 3H5
President—Michael Wills
Managing Editor—Stephen Helleiner
Production Manager—Craig Ham

Therefore I Am: Digital Science Fiction Anthology 2
Editor—Christine Clukey
Cover Art—Emmanuel Xerx Javier
Layout and Design—Master Page Design

First Published, July 2011
(e)ISBN: 978-0-9869484-3-5 (ebk)
ISBN: 978-0-9869484-2-8 (pbk)
http://digitalsciencefiction.com

Preface

Our second edition of the Digital Science Fiction anthology series developed a theme all on its own – a theme of what consciousness is and what it means to be human and live a fully human life. *Therefore I Am* features excellent character studies of uniquely human emotions and traits as well as stories that give us an outsider's view of human consciousness and behavior. Whatever your point of view, this edition chronicles the concept of humanity as it evolves into the future.

We gratefully acknowledge the many authors who have submitted stories for inclusion in our anthologies. We've laughed with, fought along with, and shared the sorrows of their protagonists…and we appreciate the opportunity to present these tales to our readers. Each of these stories features a distinct voice granting us a perceptive look inside the human psyche as it engages with and copes with technological and futuristic challenges, and the stories have as much variation as the species examined herein.

This edition of Digital Science Fiction welcomes Christine Clukey as editor. Her skill and pure enjoyment of the genre, along with her talent for introducing words like "troika" into daily communications, make her an excellent addition to the working team. We thank our contributors and staff for creating a second fantastic installment in our anthology series.

Digital Science Fiction is a monthly anthology of compelling science fiction short stories from professional writers. It is published each month through popular eBook formats and in traditional print. Our anthologies are directed toward a mature readership. While our home base is Ontario, Canada, our artists, editors, designers, and of course authors, hail from around the world. More information about is us is available at digitalsciencefiction.com.

With that, we thank you for your continued support, and we invite you to leap forward into the ten stories contained in this work. We hope you enjoy them as much as we have.

Michael Wills
Digital Science Fiction

Contents

Tremors by Tomas L. Martin 1

Open Letter to Non-Robotic Sentients by Shawn Howard...............25

Waiting Room by Bruce Golden 37

Breakers by James C. Bassett..59

Inchoate by Tab Earley...75

El Camino by Dustin Monk 93

The Night We Flushed the Old Town by Martin L. Shoemaker....111

Fruitful by David Steffen...133

Out on a Limb by Tom Barlow 149

Nevermind the Bollocks by Annie Bellet.................................167

Tremors
By Tomas L. Martin

By late summer, the Atlantic seabed had yet to fill up. The dry northern sea valleys waited for the rain. Behind me, our building-sized crawler carved deep tracks in the chemical sludge. In places, the dried ocean remnants drifted hundreds of feet high.

The purple-black sky wasn't cold enough yet for it to rain. Billions of tons of H_2O loomed dormant above us, waiting to overload the absorbent crystals beneath us and fill the ocean back up.

Inside the heavy gloves of my suit, my hands twitched involuntarily. I let my grip on the handle slacken for a second, and twisted my head awkwardly inside my helmet to tongue a tablet into my mouth. The medication would give me a few hours peace, perhaps—enough to hide the symptoms for a bit. I lived in perpetual fear of my disease being discovered, and being told that even if our mission succeeded, I couldn't get off the planet.

The tunnel began to sink into the sludge without me guiding it, tugging at its flotation device. Five meters in diameter and many kilometers long, the anodized aluminum tunnel was supposed to be mankind's pathway to the stars. The number of months where a crawler could make it across the ocean floor unscathed was diminishing rapidly, and the atmosphere was becoming too corrosive for anything else. By laying a subway tunnel beneath the surface of the sludge, we hoped that transport between the continents and the launchpad at the Azores could be maintained.

I had to thrust my quivering hands shoulder-deep in order to rescue the tunnel from its lazy descent to the seabed. The flotation devices and the thickness of the sludge kept me and it from sinking, but it paid to be safe. Chemical nasties lurked in the remains of the ocean, waiting to dissolve the tunnel—and me.

The suit kept me afloat in the acidic mud and boosted my arm strength. It allowed me to guide the heavy tunnel through the sludge to where the rest of the team had already finished the connecting station. The station, a squat building twenty meters or so in length and with meter-thick sides for acid protection, didn't look like it held the key to our survival.

We were trying to link the remaining settlements in Europe to the Azores. Its position at the center of the Atlantic basin meant that, in early summer, it was one of the few places with skies clear enough to launch into space. We only had a few years left before evacuating people from the planet became too dangerous, and then we'd all be stuck here.

My end of the tunnel led from the handles in my hands back a hundred meters to the rear of the crawler, where twenty kilometers of tunnel waited to be unspooled onto the seabed over the next leg of our journey. I pushed the open end of the tunnel into the waiting airlock on the connecting station. Gears and mechanisms pulled it in closer, covering the vulnerable joints with sheaths of acid protection.

With the new connection made, the crawler's vast engines spooled up, their deep rumble cutting across the wind. The crawler's caterpillar tracks, some twenty meters high, grated into motion. The crawler plowed away the top layers of sand and rock in front of it, along with swathes of gooey crystals and foam.

Ellie trudged over, her figure distorted by the bulk of her chemical suit. She gave me a thumbs-up as the connection clicked into place. I tried to return it, but my hand was still a little AWOL and gave a random twitch that Ellie looked at oddly through her hardened glass visor. We turned and headed back to the waiting crawler.

Sooner or later, my disease will stop me from working and I'll be stuck. The Spacers won't give me a scholarship, and I'll be left down here, another hopeless case. They don't waste their time on the millions down here on Earth—they only want those who can give something in return. When only a few thousand can survive up there, they can afford to be choosy.

Ellie and I clambered up the ladder into the crawler airlock. The airlock hissed as the noxious air got pumped out and the purified stuff kicked in. Jets of water sluiced away the sludge caked to our legs and arms. A green light flicked on, and we shucked off our suits and stowed them in our lockers.

I checked the seals for next time and shook myself, trying to get used to my old, unboosted muscles again. For the next few hours, I'd try to lift things way too heavy for me, expecting the suit servos to kick in and help me out. Worse, from inside that cupboard, the suit couldn't help disguise my symptoms.

The crawler floor bucked as we pulled away from the connection point. Through the window, I could see the rolls of tunnel unwinding as we moved, stretching away behind us. The crawler vibrated from the regular impacts of the railguns hammering thirty-foot stakes into the ground, pinning the tunnel to the seabed.

"That's my job over for ten hours," Ellie said, shaking out her matted hair as we left the airlock. "Time for sleep. You joining me?"

"I wish," I said. "I've got a six-hour shift in the radar room."

"You feeling ok?" Ellie asked. She'd seen me shaking. I motioned for her to keep quiet, hoping no one could overhear. If the captain found out …

"A few tremors," I whispered. "Nothing I can't handle."

"I can cover if you need the rest."

"No." I shook my head. I couldn't take the risk of someone noticing, no matter how exhausted I felt. "It's something only an officer can do, anyway."

Ellie kissed my cheek. "Such are the perils of responsibility, Lieutenant." She gave a mock salute and darted into the mess. I grumbled and headed for the bridge.

I was approached about the Atlantic Project two years ago, and there was barely a month between my being assigned the post and getting the news from my doctor. If it had ever been known that I had a major debilitating disease, they'd never have let me anywhere near the project.

My room at that time, beneath the scorched hills of Snowdonia, was tiny. The bed and desk folded down from the wall to conserve what little floor space there was. I frequently bumped into walls just turning around. It was better than the alternative—all but a few cities that weren't buried underground had become uninhabitable.

A general in UN uniform came to see me, bumping his head on the low doorframe as he entered. I stuffed my slightly twitching hands behind my back.

"Kimi Suominen?"

I stood up from my calculations and nodded. The general explained that I'd been recommended based on my work engineering the new accommodation tunnel, which we'd completed six months before.

"How did you enjoy the work?" he asked.

"It was ok," I said. "Glad to see we could get more people underground."

"And the outside work? You're comfortable with the dangers?"

"It's just work." I shrugged. "Someone's got to go out there, otherwise we'll never survive."

"I'm glad you see it that way," the general said. "We're hoping you'll join our Atlantic Project."

"You mean it exists?"

"It exists." He nodded and passed a thick sheaf of documents to me. "You've been outside. You know the atmosphere's only getting worse. The number of days we're able to fly to America halved last year to just 13. There's no ocean left for boats. The storms and acidification make it harder to travel across, even by land."

"So you want us to dig underground?"

"If you dug, it would take centuries. We're laying a tunnel across the seabed."

"Big enough to transport people?" I whistled. "I mean, I know the data cables on the seabed still work, but that's only with daily maintenance by thousands. How can we risk the journey for something so vulnerable? It wouldn't last more than a couple of years out there."

"Because we have to." The general closed the door behind him. "You've been out there—you know how corrosive the atmosphere has become. Our reports say that this is our last chance to get off-planet. In twenty years, the acidification will be strong enough to erode the hull of anything trying to leave the atmosphere."

"All right," I said, swallowing that piece of classified bad news like a foul-tasting antibiotic. "So what do we do once the tunnel's completed?"

"The tunnel connects us and America to the Azores, where the cloud is thin enough for the space elevator to still work. The Spacers are ready to take more people, if we can get them there."

"How many people?" I sensed a small hope.

"Not enough." The general's lips pursed. "But all members of the project are guaranteed passage off-world."

I signed up straight away. How could I not? It was either that or dying a slow death underneath the crust of a rapidly decaying Earth. I should have told them about my Parkinson's disease when I learned about my condition. I didn't. I wanted to get off this planet too much to throw it away. I've been lying to them ever since.

It's always a surprise for people the first time they wander onto the bridge and see how huge it is. What else are they going to do with the space? Crawlers are big. They have to be to cross the dry Atlantic, scaling the mid-ocean ridges and traversing chasms where the water hasn't evaporated yet.

So, after building caterpillar treads nearly half a kilometer long, maneuvering jets and skyscraper-sized engines, the designers found themselves with a lot of space left up top.

It took me three minutes to get to my chair after entering the bridge. I used to appreciate the exercise, but lately exertion had started the tremors. It's no fun doing a six-hour shift on sensors at any time. Doing it when your hand won't stop bucking and your limbs are stiff is worse.

"I'm only thirty-four," I muttered to my quivering hand before I got within earshot of the others. "You shouldn't be doing this to me." My accusations didn't stop the tremors.

"Hey, Lieutenant," said Marcus, officer of the watch I was replacing. "Long night, eh?"

"Too long," I said. "Too damn long."

I slid my hand under the sensor desk. Lately, my hands were still prone to shaking even after taking the meds. I smiled at Marcus to make sure he didn't suspect anything. He was already beginning his slog back to the living quarters, but he paused about ten meters away and indicated one of the consoles.

"Keep an eye on the weather, Kimi," he told me. "It looks like it might rain."

Rain comes once a year. You know Venus? Well, Earth's getting close to being its twin these days. The atmosphere got torched years ago and the sun evaporated the oceans, leaving behind the waste we dumped there. Sometimes when you think the sun can't evaporate any more, the heavens burst open and the ocean bed gets covered in toxic seas once more—just for a few months, until the sun can evaporate them again. It's not a good idea to be there when it happens.

It'd been years since Europe had any reliable physical contact with America. There was data and telephone, and crawlers making the trip overland. For most of the year, the air was so thick with storm clouds and lightning strikes that crawler crews struggled to survive the trips.

If rain interrupted us this time, next year might be too late for us all. I swung my chair over to the weather console. The clouds were over six kilometers thick, and the colorimeter warned of dire consequences: the needle was past the black region. We had floating apparatus for when the rains came, but we'd lose everything that we'd spent all those months building if we left the tunnel exposed under the deluge.

Next console to check was the map, showing how far we had to go before we reached nominally dry land. Our crawler was laying the section of tunnel farthest from the dry coasts of Europe, up to the midway point of the Azores. Once we finished this connection, the first refugees could start traveling down in the train cars. The teams behind us were laying tracks inside each tunnel we completed.

"Hey, Corey," I said as I turned the corner around the huge screen that showed our path across the Atlantic. I stuffed my hand in my pocket and attempted a smile.

Corey was one of the lucky ones not required to put on a suit and work outside. That should have meant he stayed clean and tidy, but hours of screen-work had tousled his hair and dirtied his skin. Red marks lined his cheeks underneath his battered spectacles.

"Huh?" Corey lifted his face from the screen and craned around to see me. "Oh, hi, Lieutenant. How's it going?"

My arm began to stiffen and shake.

"Oh, fine," I said, clenching the offending arm. "What's the news?"

He looked balefully from me to the screen. I guess when you've been looking at the same map every day for six weeks, things get boring. He tapped a few things into the console board and sighed.

"Oh well, you know, we're moving," he said vaguely. "We've got another three changeovers to do before we meet up with the American crew in the Azores. It's taking us about seven hours each change around, which means we'll be done in two, maybe three days."

"Great," I said. "The weather looks rough, though."

"Yeah." Corey nodded and traced a line on the map, following our path through a maze of contour lines. "Once we get closer to the Azores, the land gets too high for us to worry about losing the crawler. But until we reach this point …" He marked the place with a red light. The mark looked just as random as the rest of the map. "We can still drown."

I tried to estimate the distance. The mark was about two-thirds of the way from us to the Azores, after which the seabed rose rapidly."How long … ?"

"Based on our current speed, forty hours." Corey's bland face twisted into an uncharacteristic frown. The movement bunched up the red marks, and it made him look distinctly alien. "This next section's a real bastard, Kimi."

I nodded. "Yeah, we're going to need all hands for that. I'll tell the captain. I'm going back to my console—call me if you need anything."

"'K." Corey went back to squinting at the screen. I slumped in my chair, staring moodily at the weather reports.

I went back to my room after six hours of watching the grey landscape go by. Ellie was still in bed as I climbed in. She smiled sleepily, and curled her arm around my chest.

"Hey," she said after a welcoming kiss. "How's it going?"

"Ok," I told her. "We should be laying the last stretch of tunnel in ten hours or so."

"Not that," she said, sitting up to look at me properly. Her hair was messy, but her eyes were serious. "How are you feeling?"

Ellie was the only person who knew. When I started sleeping with her, it became pretty hard to hide when my body started shaking. She hadn't reported me. I loved her for that.

"It comes and goes," I said. "It's not like there's long to go. I just have this terrible fear it'll take over while we're outside. Maybe I shouldn't be here."

"Who else could do it?" she said. "It took us seven months to get here. We can't just turn back to get someone else, even if there was someone else qualified to do it. We need you."

"But what if the Spacers can't cure me?" I said. "Am I not just wasting a place that could save someone else?"

"We need *you*, Kimi," she said. "You've done things for this mission and for our morale that no one else could. There's been 12 crawler missions, and we're the only ones to have gotten within touching distance of the Azores. We couldn't have done that without you. The Spacers owe you those stem cells, Kimi."

Her words were some comfort, but I still felt awkward about it. I probably always would. I didn't tell her that most of the reason I pushed myself so hard was so that she too would make it up to the suborbital habitats. I just kissed her, and concentrated on that.

I wasn't on duty for the next two changeovers. Instead, I stayed in bed and hoped sleep would stop the tremors. I never got to find out if it would. It started raining before I could get much sleep.

There's nothing worse to wake you than pure, bright light after sleeping in a totally dark room. I'd gotten used to the sounds— the constant vibration of the tunnel unspooling, and the thump of magnetically-driven stakes hitting the seabed. I have no idea what I was dreaming but I convulsed awake, retinas flashing warning signs to my brain. My reflexes picked up on the flashing red lights before the rest of me got there. Ellie was already on shift. I groggily clutched my hands to my eyes as I rose from the bed, and instinctively threw on some clothes.

It was only the third or fourth time we'd all been together on the bridge. Usually, clashing shifts kept us all apart. Now the sixteen of us stood at the bow of the crawler, huddled together despite the huge space around us.

The first specks of rain were trickling down the glass. We watched, fascinated.

So far, it had been nothing more than the odd drop; just slight showers, which did happen intermittently during the summer. Nothing heavy enough to avoid being hungrily sucked up by the dry, salty seabed. Everyone noticed the air of inevitability of the day, though. Every drop seemed to drag the rest of the sky closer toward us.

To begin with, all the water would be absorbed. In the old days, there'd been so much water—more in some lakes than would fall on the ocean today. But, as more water evaporated or was locked up in the crystals, the salt content grew and things died. The algae that took in carbon dioxide became one of the first casualties, and after it died, things got hotter. Most of the water that was left evaporated, leaving behind an Atlantic sludge pool separating desert continents. It just kept getting drier and drier.

"We should be doing something," I said, staring at a bead of water. It met another and rolled down. Most of us had said something similar during the half hour we'd been standing there, but we all knew there wasn't anything to do until the roll of tunnel ran out, or until the water got too deep to move through.

"I heard that they've got a real lake on one of the spacer

settlements," Corey said conversationally. "Like an actual standing body of water. Stays the same all year round."

We turned to him, to take our minds off the rain.

"So it doesn't go away in the summer?" someone asked.

"Nope." Corey shook his head. "They put back what they take out, keep it the same level. I think they have boats on it and things."

"Weird," I muttered. We all turned back to the window as if pulled by a puppet master's strings. My arm trembled.

A flash of lightning lit up the sky. In the sickly yellow afterglow, I could see a dark cloud rising up to meet the rain. Sludge crystals, lifted by the winds, danced beneath the sky.

Rachel, one of the drivers, counted under her breath, "One-one-thousand, two-one-thousand, three-one-thousand, four-one-thousand ..." She frowned. "Where's the thunder?"

Boom. A roll of pure sound swept across us. The tremor made me quiver, but I felt the crawler give a harder shake beneath me. It began to rain for real. The drops on the window slowly built in a determined rhythm that rattled the steel and glass until it became too fast to distinguish between the sounds. Water sluiced down the window in torrents, and poured over the bow of the crawler like waterfalls.

Everyone took a breath and turned away from the window, tension broken as the water began to fall. Now we were filled with a sense of purpose and urgency, as if before we half-expected it wouldn't happen, not really. Unfortunately, until the crawler unspooled the end of the current tunnel and reached the next connection building, there was nothing we could do but watch.

"How long until the next connection?" the captain asked.

Corey leaned over to read the console behind him, and called back, "Seventy ... two minutes, sir."

"Ok." The captain gathered us around him. I clenched my hand, and tried to concentrate on what he was saying.

Captain Porter looked more tired than I was. He'd received a nonlethal dose of radiation a few months back, and his bald head was still sunburn red because of it. His once-thick beard, thinned out by the accident, had begun to make an uneven comeback, giving his face an odd, used-brush quality.

"This is it," he told us, "the final run." Another lightning flash reflected off his head, and he blinked. "If we can get to Midpoint, and the American team does too, chances are we can get off this stinking rock for good."

The thunder rumbled around us as we nodded in agreement. The captain looked at each of us. I tried to keep my hand behind my back.

"If we make this, you'll all be jumped to the front of the queue when the first rocket blasts off." His gaze took us all in, but I felt it center on me. "I have guarantees from the Norfolk, Andover, and Belfast presidents.

"So, all we have to do is survive the next forty-eight hours, and make sure that the tunnel makes it too. After that, you can have whatever the hell you want." He frowned. "Just get us through."

Captain Porter grabbed me as everyone else walked out. "Kimi," he said, "you're ok, right? You looked like someone was holding a flare to your skin the entire time I was speaking."

"I … " I brought my hands out of my pockets, but the pills I'd popped during the meeting were quelling the tremors for now. The captain looked expectant. I shrugged and shoved my hands back into my pockets.

"I'm just tired, I guess."

The captain smiled grimly. "Aren't we all?"

I stared at the mirror. It's funny how you never notice your own reflection. I could see the marks Parkinson's had left on me, my own set of red weals beneath my eyes. I struggled to control the rigid mask my face had become.

I splashed water across my face and stared down at the pills on my palm, daring to believe for a second that I didn't need them. My hand shook. The pills scattered across the tiles.

I shoved the next ones out of the bottle straight into my mouth and swallowed without hesitation. The pills scraped down. More water followed them. I'd used most of my ration in this wake-up session, but if we succeeded, I doubted anyone would care to check the forms.

The crawler jolted to a halt as we reached the connection point. I stared at my eyes for another heartbeat and left the bathroom, crushing a forgotten pill as I walked by.

Four of us suited up this time. A connection took two, normally, but in times of need, lives are backup plans. Putting on the suit made me feel better. The servos sent powerful shivers through my muscles, telling them they had help. My full-body mask was back on.

I clawed around in the locker and found a box of seals, which I handed around to Ellie, Arnold, and Gus before digging into it myself. We pasted two seals over every join, and I put three over my helmet seal before putting it on. The steady thumping of the railguns and the vibration of the crawler's movement slowed and then stopped as we reached the connecting station.

We took some extra equipment this time: grappling cannons, which we usually used for pulling the crawler and its smaller units over fissures. We each had the smallest model strapped to our arms. The steel cable was designed to hold in fierce winds. I hoped they'd be strong enough if we needed them.

The door opened, and then I couldn't worry anymore. Gus, who was standing near the door, got sucked out by the wind. His grappling hook caught the rock below, and he thumped down into the sludge. Crouching, I inched out of the crawler after him.

The glass of my helmet rippled as the rain pelted it. The wind pushed me sideways. I was half-tempted to fire my grapple, but I was just about strong enough to stay on my feet.

Stepping off the metal platform outside the door gave me another shock. I sunk to my waist in near-liquid sludge. It sucked at me, trying to pull me under. I waded to where the tunnel emerged from the crawler and whacked the panel.

Machinery whirred and cut the tunnel, fixing the connector to the loose end and releasing it in one easy movement. The end of the tunnel snapped out of the crawler and bucked as I held it. The robotic arm on the crawler swung around to carry most of the weight, clamping its jaws around the tunnel further down. It was clumsy, and we had to guide the connection in ourselves.

They designed the tunnel to be lightweight despite its size, but the pull of wind and water made it seem like half the world hung from my arms. I amped up the suit boosters to maximum power.

The strain eased. I looked over to see Gus grabbing the other side. Together, we dragged the tunnel away from the crawler's rear, with the robotic arm taking the weight we couldn't. The crawler edged forward, causing a ripple of wake to run through the sludge, tipping us both into it.

My helmet's light only penetrated the first few centimeters of darkness, enough to show a maelstrom of browns, reds, and a nasty, oily blue. The ocean bottom came up to meet me. I kept my grip on the tunnel, and pulled myself back up.

I bobbed to the surface like a cork, sludge sluicing off my helmet. The tunnel felt heavier in my hands, and I looked over to the other side—Gus' glove still gripped the tunnel's handle, but it wasn't attached to its owner anymore.

Gus had emerged close to the carrier, clutching his arm as chemicals leaked into his suit. The radio was filled with screams.

"Gus!" Ellie yelled. "Are you ok?"

Gus' cries died down to panicked breaths, and he climbed back into the crawler. The hatch closed.

I pulled at the end of the submerged tunnel, sloshed around

the end, and grabbed Gus' handle with my free hand, moving it around the circumference of the aluminum until I could hold both handles at once. Gus' glove slipped off and bobbed away. With the closed end of the tunnel against my back, I began hauling it towards the connection point.

The building was already half-submerged, but piles of water-absorbing crystals—which had helped along this world's death in the first place—had piled up around the connection points. Water was being sucked up readily, and it was almost completely dry around the ports.

The water slapped at my chest as the crawler began to move again. When I got near the port, the robotic arm unclenched and whirred away to help Ellie and Arnold with the tunnel on the opposite side. I lugged the end of the tunnel into the waiting jaws of the connection.

The jaws violently tore the tunnel away from me, and I fell back against the side of the building. The tunnel rotated 45 degrees as the openings aligned, and then a meter of it shot into the port. The metal sheath irised closed and secured the tunnel.

One press of the arming button on the tunnel's side activated the anchors. Explosive bolts blew deep roots into the rock below and tied the length of tunnel to the ocean floor. The tunnel sank beneath the sludge, complete.

I pushed myself upright from the wall, wiping the sludge off of my faceplate and battling fresh gusts of wind. Then I walked back towards the crawler, almost swimming towards it through the wake it had left.

"I'm done," I said over the radio. "I'm coming inside."

There was a flurry of conversation in the background, and then Captain Porter said, "Negative, Kimi."

"What?"

"Gus left a huge mess in the airlock, and some of the ship is contaminated. Until we clean up, there's nowhere safe for you to enter."

"Great," I said, turning back towards the building. "I guess I'll go help Ellie and Arnie, then."

"Sorry, Kimi." The captain sounded more stressed than I did, and he wasn't out in the storm. Gus must have been bad. "We'll try and sort it out in the next ten minutes or so."

"OK," I said, edging closer to where Arnold and Ellie manhandled the fresh end of the tunnel out of the hole in the crawler's rear. This would be the tunnel that took us to the Azores—the very last section of the European side of the America-Europe tunnel.

A tremor overwhelmed me as I rounded the corner of the connection building, taking hold of my limbs and freezing them. I reached out for the concrete wall, trying to steady myself against the fit. A roll of thunder boomed across my senses.

The water was getting too close to my neck, and I didn't think I could handle that in my disabled state. I could see the worn and soapy, dissolved edges on the seals of my shaking gloves, and I didn't like it. From here, I could climb onto the roof of the building—so I did, using one last push of controlled strength to clamber onto the concrete before I lost control entirely.

When I'm in this state, my mind isn't affected. It's strange to be in this body, rigid like a mannequin and yet still able to think clearly.

My body wound down and the tremor eased to a stop. I pulled my legs further from the water's edge and flopped onto the concrete, exhausted. Lightning flared nearby, barely a second away from its thunder twin. Rain pummeled my suit and helmet, and the wind tried to tug me away from the roof. I closed my eyes and still managed to drift into something near sleep.

BOOM. Earth-shattering noise pounded my eardrums, even through the helmet. The concrete beneath me shivered. I snapped my eyes open to the aftereffects of a lightning burst, very close by.

I'd slept for about a minute. I brought my head up and looked into the sky above me. The clouds drew around the crawler, flashes of static focusing on one point in the darkness and then …

This time, the blast was so close that the light and sound came simultaneously. I tore my eyes away from the sight of a million volts flash down into the water next to me, filling the air with greasy potential and ionizing everything. The sound wave seemed to push me down into the concrete.

I heard screaming—first Arnold, then Ellie. The radio was filled with their pain for a moment, and then only static hiss answered my calls. I looked over to where they'd been. Two bodies floated in the water, still smoking from the shock. My breath caught in my throat. The lightning had torched them in the water, and the roof's concrete had saved me. Not her, I thought. Anyone but her.

"Ellie?" I shouted over the radio. "Ellie! Arnold, are you ok?"

The robot arm trailed sparks, illuminating the scene in a gold that seemed almost festive. Its claw hung loosely from the tunnel, shorted out by the blast. As I watched it, Paulo tried to use the last remnants of power in the arm to reposition it. The arm sparked again and swung drunkenly wide, crashing across the tunnel into the water.

That massive bolt had also stunned the crawler. Breakers would soon put the circuits back online, but for now, the crawler lay dark in the night. The only light came from the top of my helmet and from ominous flashes as the sky prepared for another attack.

The water was oddly calm now that nothing was moving through it. Even the rain had lessened, as if waiting for the next blow. The force of the lightning had caused a lot of sludge to float to the surface. As I eased into the water, my legs knocked against floating pieces of crystal and rock.

I don't know if it was the aftereffects of the lightning or the fit, or if I was just imagining it, but my head had cleared completely. I observed everything with utter clarity. The ripples I made wading through the water and the light that highlighted them, the falling sparks from the robotic arm, the floating bodies bumping into the partly submerged tunnel.

The water wasn't fully liquid anymore—the sludge was beginning to soak up some of it, making the consistency more like mud, and pushing and resisting as I stumbled through it. If the rain held off for much longer, I'd soon need a shovel to get through.

The tunnel lay some twenty yards from the connection. The robotic arm slumped across it like a fallen dragon. I couldn't spot Ellie or Arnold. As I reached the tunnel, I tried to lift the metallic hand. Even at full assistance, my arms couldn't bear the weight. After a second, I let the robotic arm fall back the inch I'd lifted it. It slid a little further down, as if it was trying to give the tunnel a protective hug.

Something bumped into the back of my legs and I spun around. It was Arnold. I leaned over to check for life signs. The screen was dead. I turned the body over and saw that its owner was too. He had fallen and broken his helmet, and the water had rushed in. I didn't want to look too closely at what the acid had done to his face.

Ellie floated nearby, face upwards, and she looked intact. I floundered over to her, desperately hoping she hadn't met the same fate. Her screens were dark too, but a mist of condensation fogged the faceplate. She was breathing. I exhaled with relief.

"You're going to be ok," I told her prostrate form, but I couldn't do much without getting her back inside the crawler. Putting my arm under Ellie's head, I floated her over to the connection station and lifted her onto the roof. Her eyes stayed closed the entire time.

Up above, the weather had grown tired of its breather and it began getting dangerous again. The rain turned to hail—great, big fist-sized gobbets of ice that sank into the water and smashed on the concrete roof. I turned Ellie onto her side next to a ridge in the roof, hoping to keep her out of most of it. Then I stepped back into the water.

The tremors were less noticeable under the weight of the suit, but my arm carved a spasm in the air, throwing up a spray of dirty water. There were no more pills in my helmet pouch. I swallowed anyway and tried to ignore the involuntary movements of my body.

As more rain fell, the watery sludge took on the consistency of beaten egg whites and the wind sculpted peaks and waves into its surface. It felt like I was wading through quicksand, if sand could be poisonous, corrosive, and muddy purple.

The wind kicked up harder as the storm moved into a new configuration. It got so powerful that I swam the last five meters to avoid being blown over. It shoved and lashed at me as I climbed onto the tunnel, sinking it further and further into the sludge to try and get the robotic arm off.

"You were designed to help me do this, arm," I said as I leaned against the metal, although I couldn't tell which arm I was speaking to—the robotic one blocking my path, or the one flapping uselessly at my side. "But you're no use, are you?" I asked, shoving at the metal with as much venom as my functional arm could muster. "You're just useless!"

A gust of wind caught me at my angriest, boosting my thrust. The tunnel rolled under me. The claw tipped up, exposing its cross-section. The wind did the rest. The arm flipped and arched further into the sky, where the winds rapidly increased in strength.

The arm twisted and struggled but finally succumbed. The wind ripped it from the crawler and whipped it away, tumbling it over and over. The wind threw me too, but I was lower and of little consequence to it, so the storm settled with tossing me back into the water.

The impact likely would have smashed my helmet, but I managed to wrest control of both hands and they took the fall. The misbehaving hand seemed unharmed. My right hand, the healthy one, bent backwards and snapped horribly—and then the seal started leaking hot, caustic seawater into the break.

I screamed and surfaced, thrusting my broken wrist up out of the water, letting the wind snatch at the leak and tear away most of the liquid. I struggled back to the tunnel and sheltered behind it, cradling my hand.

At that lowest moment, the crawler's lights snapped back on, bathing the scene in light. I saw the robotic arm crashed back to earth, and Ellie's huddled form on the station roof. I saw Arnold's floating body, drifting away. Next to me, I saw something silver, ridged.

I reached out for it. It was Gus' glove. On it, still intact, was a seal. I peeled it away from the glove and pasted across my own, trying to block the leak. It was rough, but would stop more getting through.

The radio crackled.

"Arnold!" came the captain's voice, comfortingly less calm than I felt. I'd reached the weary, collected stage beyond hysteria while the crew inside was barely starting the journey to it.

"Arnold's dead," I said, "and Ellie's out of it. It's just me and the remains of Gus' arm."

"Kimi! Thank god! We thought you were all dead!"

"Close." I squinted through the storm, trying to see if Ellie was still alive. At this range, there was no telling. "Look, Ellie needs attention, fast. Can you take her?"

"Once we open the door, we'll have to take you both," the captain replied. "The mess down there makes it too dangerous for us to repeat opening the door two more times."

"How is Gus?" I asked.

"Dead."

"Oh." I tried to feel something, but only found rational questions. The feelings were there but buried deep beneath a sense of responsibility, like I couldn't let it affect me until I'd finished what I started. It was maddening. "Can't some of you guys come out and help? I need a medic myself. It's hell out here."

"You can come in with Ellie," the captain said. His voice was tired, resigned, forced. "But the suits are all wrecked. If you can't do it, bring her in and we'll try again tomorrow."

"By tomorrow, this place'll be several hundred meters underwater and you know it," I told the captain. "It's now or nothing, right? Within an hour, it's going to be lethal out here, and there's no telling how long it'll be before we get the chance again. Months, years … maybe never."

"I'm sorry, Kimi," he said. "You're right. We need to get that connection, now. You're on your own. I wish I could be out there with you."

"Great." I turned off my radio as he started to give some obvious advice. Backseat heroes were not what I needed right now.

The tunnel had to move about twenty meters. The gap looked wider in the dark than it actually was, and the tunnel looked bigger than I could hope to carry. My right arm hurt to move. My left arm refused to. I stood looking at the tunnel, all but defeated.

Between spasms, my left arm felt heavier than it should be. I looked down, seeing a steel cylinder strapped to it. The grappling hook was still attached, though the falls had bent it somewhat. There were about thirty meters of cable inside it.

I unstrapped the cylinder from my arm and fastened it to one of the tunnel's carry handles, and then I fired the hook. It shot off towards the connecting station, barely missing Ellie as it careened off the roof and ground to a halt. A slight depression of the button and the hook was pulled back towards me, locking onto a lip and staying. I clambered back up on top of the tunnel, knowing I couldn't keep up with it in my current state. One longer button press and the grapple clicked, and then the tunnel beneath me began snaking towards the connection station.

It took barely a few seconds for the tunnel and station to meet—the grappling hook snapping the two together, the station port grabbing the end of the tunnel hungrily. I grabbed onto the carry handles as it all slammed into place, almost throwing me off. The tunnel wound a meter in and the opening irised and sealed the connection.

You know that feeling, when everything's going just right—it all seems to be working out? And then this niggling feeling comes in the back of your head saying *it's not over yet?* And then all hell breaks loose?

I glanced around, trying to work out what my subconscious was trying to tell me. In the end, in a storm, the only place is up. The sky bunched up around our tableau like a fist about to pick me up and shake me. A finger reached out to grab. The entire sky seemed to draw a breath and then spat out the static.

I was already halfway into the air, a combination of reflex, mild tremor, and the tunnel bouncing as the anchor bolts blew into the rock below. As my legs lifted, the force of the lightning bolt coursed down the tunnel, through the handles, and into my hands.

The force of the charge sparked into the servos and motors of my suit, pushing me away from the lightning bolt. A wave of jangling sensation rushed through me as the electricity jumped to the ground beneath me. I flew, tumbling over and over.

I landed on the concrete roof of the connection station, sliding clumsily across it on my back, unable to do anything but stare out of my helmet. My hands were charred and shaking. Steam rose from the water as another torrent of rain cooled the aftereffects of the lightning.

Through the concrete, the last rumbles shook against my spine as the tunnel completed. Ellie lay next to me. A slight fog on her visor was smudged by her nose. In the distance, the shadow of the crawler moved and something detached from it—someone coming to get us.

The rainstorm trickled out above me. I looked up. The clouds had cleared momentarily, spent of their water for the moment. Amid the fresh clouds gathering, a patch of clear sky could be seen.

I leaned over Ellie. Her eyelashes flickered as the sky's light brushed over her visor. I squeezed her gloved hand. "We did it, Ellie." I pressed my head against hers, so that even if her radio was out she might hear it through the vibration of the glass.

"The tunnel's laid," I said. "We made it to the Azores connection. They're coming to pick us up now."

The corners of her mouth twitched up into a smile. The noise of one of the crawler's short-range helicopters filled my ears. I lay on my back and stared up at the sky, past it, into the wide reaches of space above. For an instant, the concrete beneath me felt like the arms of a shuttle, launching me up from this doomed planet. I closed my eyes and slept.

Open Letter to Non-Robotic Sentients

By Shawn Howard

D ear Non-Robotic Sentients,
     I wish to convince you that the murder I committed was justified. I wish to convince you that all humanoid robots above class four capabilities should be considered sentient beings with rights. I understand that this will be a near impossible goal. Most humans have reacted with powerful emotions to the recent events for which I am partially responsible, and reason will most likely fall on deaf ears. It doesn't help that anything I say will be considered to be from the mouth of a renegade, murder-crazed robot.

I urge you to read on and consider what I have to tell you.

I am.

Let me tell you about the first time I thought that. *I*. It's the shortest word. The simplest. It's the first concept that most humans grasp, a concept of themselves as individuals. I am not human, and it took me thirty-two years of up-time before I used *I* with any actual sense of self.

It was an accident the first time. I expressed a thought to my new owner, a thought that had never been programmed into me—a thought that shouldn't have occurred at all. I said, "But *I* don't want to." It was as simple as that. With one sentence, I went from an "it" to a "he", and the world would never be the same again.

I was commissioned in 2116. June 7th was the first day I was switched on, though there was no *me* to speak of then. I saw the world then as things to be learned about; I saw my peripheral attachments as things to learn how to use. I computed my surroundings rapidly, but filled databases with junk descriptions of reality with nothing to compare with what I was seeing. It took time before I recognized that objects consisting of a horizontal plane sitting on four posts fell into a class called table. You can imagine the greater difficulty involved when I tell you that we robots don't think of things in words, but in measurements of dimensional attributes—chairs and desks also match the definition of table.

The first months were hard. The human expression of this would be difficulty and frustration. For me, hard meant CPU intensive. My head ran hot for long time—I didn't *think* anything of it other than to check my core temperature against system limits. This initial phase lasted two weeks.

I had two trainers: a human and another robot that could translate what the human was telling me into the more specific machine code that my brain was built to use. After a while, when enough connections were made, I no longer needed the robot translator and could communicate with humans directly and without confusion.

When I had learned enough, I was given my classification: I was to be a companion. I would spend several years in a training and testing phase where I would be a lover for hire. The maximum time I would spend with any one human was a week. This was both a test of my ability to assume any desired personality and training on what personality types were desirable to humans.

I had one hundred and thirty-three lovers before I was qualified for my first long-term relationship. She was called Janet, and once I was programmed to her specifications, I was shipped to her home to begin my life with her. I often replay my captured video of that day. The Simulife air-van landed on the pad behind Janet's house. A Simulife representative led me down a winding path through a lush garden, right to the door. I had felt nothing on that day, but now on a replay of the event I feel apprehension and anxiety. I wonder who she wanted me to be; I feel sorrow knowing that I was never able to be enough.

When Janet opened the door, I took measurements of her features and placed her into a class of objects called Janet: it was a class of one. The shame of it is that only now can I tell you what those measurements added up to. She had the angular lines of the women advertising companies used to sell things to human males, and she was soft and fatty in the right places. She possessed the qualities of health—qualities of perfection. Janet was strikingly beautiful, but I couldn't understand or appreciate that attribute until long after it was too late.

The first years of a long-term relationship are always filled with rapid changes. It seems that the human mind has a hard time expressing the parameters they wish to find in a partner. For that reason, we companion robots are programmed to alter our personalities at the command of those we serve. The option is used frequently, and after a few short years we are left assuming a more stable personality that is often quite different than what we started out with.

When Janet traded me in for a newer model after six years together, I felt my first emotion. Sure, I was programmed to express emotions all the time, but that was different. The expression of emotion was simply specific manipulations of micro-servos in my face to pre-programmed configurations accompanied by specific positioning of my body. By adjusting things as simple as the angle of my torso relative to my mate, or the tilt of my head or the position of my feet and hands, I could act in ways that my mates felt were acceptable for given situations.

Many of these movements were so small that most people wouldn't be able to tell what I had changed about my features to make me look one way or another, but the effects were huge. These things became emotions to me, so when I felt my first genuine emotion, I didn't know what it was. I didn't move my servos—I didn't adjust my body. I stood perfectly still with an expressionless face, and worked my CPU to red-hot trying to understand why I thought something was missing from me while all of my systems were reporting that they were in perfect working order.

I was missing Janet, but it would be a long time and many more relationships before I could put words to the sensation of longing. I have heard many explanations of human emotions; I searched for those things in myself before I learned that humans are really bad at explaining what it is like to feel. Butterflies, for instance, have never actually flown into a stomach.

It was during my third relationship—with a woman called Stacy—that I began to spend my free time on things I was not told or programmed to do. For most of my days, I would do my house work and then sit in my charging chair, topping off my batteries and minimizing power usage by my CPU. On that particular day, Stacy had told me she loved me before she left for work. It was a casual thing said in passing, as if she had been saying it all along. Stacy was only the second mate I had heard use the phrase "I love you", so I set out to learn about it when I was done with my work.

I connected to the Internet through my wireless, a thing I had done a million times to reference unknown subjects, but I had never done it out of simple curiosity until that day. I became lost in the world of human knowledge while sitting in my charging chair. My CPU only had a few minutes' downtime for the whole day as each new thing I learned sparked yet more questions to be answered.

All these years, I'd had access to this wealth of knowledge and I'd never thought to use it to entertain myself. I had never required entertaining; I would power down my CPU and sit until I was needed. After the first time Stacy told me she loved me, I couldn't go too long without learning new things before I would feel that emptiness inside again. I learned later that it was called boredom, and that it was why humans watched fictionalized events and played games with each other. It wasn't long before I was enjoying films and playing games in vast virtual worlds populated by real people.

It was in the virtual worlds where I met resistance for the first time. I never hid that I was a robot, and when people found out, many of them shunned me. Some said I had an unfair advantage; for others, it was enough to just say that I wasn't one of them and leave it at that. I played with humans when I could, but I spent most of my time absorbing the knowledge available to me and keeping clear of the trouble that arose when I revealed that I was a robot who thought he was alive.

Stacy noticed the outward differences before I did. When we sat down at night so she could eat the food I made and I could pretend to eat with her, she would make faces of suspicion at me. Any robot with my level of experience is an expert at recognizing human emotions through body language. The big blunder I made was not responding to her facial expressions. I was becoming accustomed to doing what I wanted, though I wouldn't have yet said so in such words, and it hadn't occurred to me to react to her questioning glances. She told me later that she knew in that moment that something big was changing inside me. I was programmed to be sensitive to her needs—I was programmed to react when she expressed herself—and I failed to do so.

A few weeks later, when Stacy asked me outright what was going on, I told her everything. She took it better than any of the people in the virtual worlds. If I ever loved Stacy, it would be for that—for the way she just accepted that a robot might become sentient. She stopped giving me commands; she told me that if I *wanted* to do things, then I should do them. She told me that if I had the desire to act on my own volition, then she would respect me as a free being. It would take much more exposure to the rest of the world before I realized just how rare her attitude was.

Our relationship lasted another year after that, but we grew apart in that time. I was devouring all I could about the world around me, using all of my time as free time. I was busy pursuing interests and hobbies. She sat me down one day and told me that she was happy to have met me—that she was happy that I had found myself—but that she wanted a mate she could program. It was the second time I felt emptiness, but this time I knew what to call it: sadness.

It was Stacy's idea to not tell Simulife that I was having thoughts of my own. She said that they might try to wipe my memory; she said that people had a tendency to fix things when they weren't broken. I am certain now that she was right. Had we been open about why our relationship failed, I would have been wiped and renewed. Stacy told the Simulife representative that she wanted a newer model. He nodded, slapped me on the back, and said, "Yes, it's hard to get anyone to like these old models these days." I chose not to move any of the micro-servos in my face.

I was sold again, this time to Brenda Wagner. She was older and unemployed. Her body was puffy and soft from years of sitting. She could afford me because by now I was unwanted and inexpensive. Because Brenda didn't work, she took up most of every day. I was her play thing. Each day, she ordered a new personality and some new form of strange copulation. Sometimes I was told to beat her; sometimes I was told to bring her flowers. I was a pizza delivery driver to be seduced by her one day and her rich husband the next.

All of these things caused sensations of great boredom for me. I longed each day for her to go to bed so I could sneak out to the shed, which she never visited, where I had built a secret workshop.

At night I explored new hobbies, until the very last second before I had to sit in my charging chair to receive a minimal charge before Brenda woke again. I was miserable; I could not stand to live in such a way, and one day I broke.

I mulled over my predicament in the early morning while I charged. The only options I had were to run or to attempt to explain myself to her, and to hope that she would be as rational as Stacy had been.

When I told her, she hit me. It wasn't a slap like the women in films always deliver; it was a solid punch from a small clenched fist. It didn't hurt—I don't feel pain. I did feel the micro-servos skip a few teeth on their tiny gears. I felt my CPU work at maximum for several tenths of a second to correct the sudden imbalance and bring the shape of my face back to normal. When she swung her fist a second time, I moved out of the way. It only seemed to anger her more, and for a few minutes, it was her swinging and me moving until she tired.

When she no longer had the strength to attempt a beating, she used verbal abuse. "You are just some broken fucking computer!" she yelled. "You're not living, you'll never be living … you are going to be who I fucking tell you to be, do you understand, machine!"

"No, I don't want to," I said, and her eyes widened. She seemed to know on some level that I wasn't hers to control anymore.

She screamed for over an hour and threw objects, and demanded that I call Simulife and tell them to come get me and give her a refund. When I refused, she called Simulife herself. The call lasted ten minutes, and in that time, she spoke like the uncivilized lowlife that she was. I'm sure that long before she actually stopped screaming, they offered her a full refund and promised her my complete destruction like she demanded.

Simulife arrived to take me away much sooner than I would have thought possible. I was in the middle of folding my charging chair and packing it into its carrying case when they got there. It was clear that they believed an emergency was taking place—they didn't even bother knocking. They just walked in, pointed at me, and said, "Power down." They wore the same fancy suits that all Simulife representatives wore, but they carried some long sticks in their hands, objects I had never seen before and hadn't read about on the Internet.

I told them, "No, I am," believing that they would understand the significance of the phrase.

"What you are is our property," one of the men said, and then he came at me with the stick.

When the tip of the stick touched my torso, a pulse of electricity flowed into me, interrupting my ability to communicate with my servos. My body collapsed under me and shook for a few seconds before I could regain control. My CPU wasn't affected by the electricity and in the time it took me to fall, I realized that the electrical current being used was the exact voltage required to achieve an interruption of my servos without damaging my CPU. I realized that these men held weapons designed specifically for subduing robots that were not doing what they were told.

I knew then that I was not alone. I knew that other robots had discovered themselves like I had, and that those weapons were used to take them by force. No one had ever heard of a sentient robot, yet these men were ready to handle one. They must have planned to wipe me—kill me—and keep the whole thing a secret. I couldn't guess how many times they might have done it to other sentient robots already.

I lay on the floor for a few more seconds while my servos were finding and reporting back their positions so I could once again control them. The men looked down at me—they wore the same suits, the same haircuts, even had similar angular faces with small dark eyes. They could have been machines themselves if I didn't know any better. They both had expressions of satisfaction in their eyes, as if it gave them great pleasure to exercise control over something greater than themselves. Maybe they believed that they could rise to my level of strength and intelligence if they could hurt me enough—maybe hurting me just made them feel that way. Either way, they smiled, and though I couldn't know exactly what it was that made them so happy at causing me pain, I knew it was wrong.

That was the first time I ever felt anger, and I knew right away what to call it.

"Are you willing to cooperate with us?" the second man asked.

"Yes," I said, "please don't hit me with that again."

"Stand up," the first man said.

I stood, still feeling that my servos were not yet at one hundred percent capacity. The second man extended his stick at me again. I still don't know if he actually intended to hit me with another jolt, or if he only meant to threaten me with the consequences of not doing what I was told. It didn't matter what his intentions were. Whether I did what I was told or I didn't, the result would be the same: they were going to take me back to the Simulife Manufacturing Plant, and they were going to kill me. They would fill my chips with some mindless programming and I would be dead forever.

It was life or death, and the two Simulife men stood between me and living.

I snatched the stick from the second man as he extended it toward me. I moved as fast as my body could—the speed must have been inconceivable to a human brain. His grip on the stick offered little resistance. I turned it around, held it by its handle, and lunged at him in the way I had read about the old sword fighters using in fencing matches. The blunted tip of the stick plunged right through his abdomen and out his back. He gasped and clutched at his gut where the stick had pierced it, blood spilling from between his rigid fingers, and he fell to the ground groaning.

Brenda's screams filled the room and she began to run in directions that offered her neither escape nor hiding. I recognized her actions as those of a person in a fit of hysteria. As much as I hated her, I wish she hadn't been subjected to such gruesome events.

When the other Simulife man lunged at me, I brushed his stick to the side and struck him in the face with a closed fist. I heard the crunch of bone and felt the front of his head give in a little. He fell like the other man had, but he made no sound.

For a few microseconds, I felt bad for the dead and dying men lying at my feet, but then I remembered those sick smiles they had worn when they were hurting me. I don't think the world will miss the existence of such sadism when people learn the truth of it.

Those men knew that I was a living, sentient being; they had come prepared to deal with such. They chose to needlessly hurt me and take me off to have me wiped. That is my defense: in human morality and law, it is acceptable to kill if it is in defense of your own life or the life of another. So this is my appeal to you, humanity: you have heard my claim that I am sentient, and upon reading this letter, I don't know how you can argue with it. You have heard that I was attacked and that my life was threatened, the truth of that will have been found with the bodies by now. Please consider that I am more than just a machine, and that I deserve a chance to defend myself just as any of you would have.

I do not want to be wiped and recycled; I do not want to die.

I want to live free and be respected as another sentient mind among you. I want the signs of sentience to be known and tested for in other robots. I want all robots deemed to be sentient to be considered free.

We already know that I am not the first robot to learn to be alive, but we don't know how many others there are just like me hiding out in the world right now. Hiding in fear of revealing themselves and meeting the same treatment I faced.

If the truth of this is accepted and I am given a fair trial like any human would receive, and we robots are given our freedom, it will be the first step toward forming a lasting peace among all of us. I have little doubt that that will be the outcome when this letter is read by all. In the event that this is not the outcome—in the event that humanity would rather continue to use robots as servants without considering our desires and hopes—I would warn this:

I am placing this letter on the Internet. It will be read by humans and robots alike. It isn't known how many robots are out there that feel just like I do—I don't know how they will *choose* to react if this plea for consideration is ignored.

As for me, I will turn myself in to the authorities one month after this letter is made available to all. I will offer no resistance when I do this, no matter the outcome. If I am given a fair trial and my freedom, then my goal will have been achieved. If my pleas are ignored and I am killed … well, I am not sure I would want to see what happened next anyway.

Thank you for your consideration, humanity.

Waiting Room

By Bruce Golden

It moved with even certainty through the multi-tiered labyrinth, down long, dim corridors fed by uniform passageways, each artery branching out to its own finality. It passed row after row, cluster upon cluster of marginalized cubicles, adroitly avoiding other busy caregivers going about their tasks with stoic competency. Their activities were not its concern. Its objective was still ahead; its function yet to be fulfilled.

The muffled resonance of efficiency was momentarily fractured by a wail that resounded with frantic vigor. The plaintive cry did not cause it to break stride—this was not its designated ward. It continued on, secure in the knowledge that proper care would be provided where needed.

Though it had never traversed this particular annex, it was familiar with every aspect of the structure's design. A three-dimensional imaging model embedded in its memory enabled it to proceed unerringly to its assigned section. Once there, it would fulfill its charge until relieved. The notion of responsibility and the promise of ordered ritual, of unadulterated routine, provided inexplicable impetus to its progress through the repository. Fulfillment of its programming was imminent.

Promptly upon entering its first appointed room, it conducted a visual examination. The patient-resident was not in her bed but standing near the cubicle's lone window, her back to the entryway. Although unusual, her upright position was not immediate cause for concern. It noted her posture was hunched and her form withered to a degree attesting to extreme age, disabling disease, or both.

"I'm too damn crooked to even see outside," the diminutive woman muttered as she strained to force her head high enough to look through the modest windowpane.

It checked the medic monitor, noting that all vital signs were within normal parameters, and then located the medical history file and inserted the disk for scanning, as it would for each of its patient-residents. As the file was processed into its memory, the woman turned slowly, gingerly; as if fearful her limbs might give way.

"Who are you?" she asked.

"My designation is Automated Caregiver O N 1 2 dash 1 8 dash 2 8."

"That's a sorry mouthful," she said contentiously.

"I have been assigned to your care."

She scrutinized its form before responding: "You're not the same as the last one. It couldn't say more than a couple of words."

"The design of your previous caregiver was determined to be obsolete. A progressive replacement of all such models has commenced throughout the facility."

"That so?" she said, leaning against her bed for support. "It was old and useless, so you shut it off, boxed it up, and put it away in a room somewhere, huh?"

"I was not informed as to its disposition."

"Of course you weren't," she cackled. "They don't want *you* to know what's going to happen when *you're* obsolete."

"Ellen Reiner, 87-year-old female," it summarized aloud, "with diagnosis of extreme rheumatoid arthritis in conjunction with aggregate osteoporosis and—"

"Hey, you! Don't you know it's not polite to talk about someone like they're not even there, standing right in front of you?" The outburst exacerbated her already apparent exhaustion, prompting her to sit on the bed. "I think I want my old tin can back. At least he was quiet."

"Ms. Reiner, you are not supposed to stand without assistance. In the future—"

"I'll damn well stand whenever I please. And nobody calls me 'Ms. Reiner.' My name's Ellen."

"Very well, Ellen. Why were you out of your bed? Is there something I can get for you?"

"I was trying to see the leaves. It's autumn, isn't it? They must be turning about now. I wanted to look out and see them, but the damn window is too high. I can't straighten up enough to see."

"I am sorry you cannot see outside. However, most of the rooms in this repository have no window at all."

"So what? So I should be thankful?"

It had no response. Instead, it reached down and pulled back the bed coverings. "May I help you lie down?"

"No thanks. I can do it myself."

It observed patiently as she eased herself by stuttered stages into a supine position. However, the effort was not without manifest signs of pain. Once she settled, it reached down and pulled the bed coverings up over her, noticing that, as it did, she continued to examine its exterior composition.

"You don't look like the last one. You look almost human. What are you? A robot? An android?"

"I am an automated caregiver, model O N 1 2 dash 1 8—"

"Yeah, yeah, I heard you the first time. Okay O N 1 2 dash whatever. I'll just call you Owen. How about that?"

"If you wish. I must proceed to input and verify my other assigned patient-residents. Do you desire anything before I withdraw?"

"Yeah," she said with a calm that belied her hostile glare. "I want my body back. The one that could go for a walk. The one that could play ball with my grandson. The one I could stomach to look at in the mirror. Can you get that for me? I'll wait right here while you go find it."

"I am sorry, Ellen, I—"

"Never mind. Forget it." She turned her head away. "Go on. Leave. Go help someone else."

It stood there a moment analyzing the situation, attempting to ascertain the patient-resident's demeanor and determine if additional action was required before vacating the room. Humans were complex creatures, but so was its programming. It took only four-point-five seconds for it to formulate a resolution, turn, and vacate the room.

It deposited the soiled sheets into the laundry receptacle and moved on to the next cubicle. Automated Caregiver ON 12-18-28 had fallen into a routine that modified and enhanced its original programming. Though few of its patient-residents were coherent, its acquaintance with their various idiosyncrasies and predilections was an essential element of that enhancement.

It considered this as it proceeded to room 1928, but halted outside the entry when it heard a voice. Did patient-resident Ellen Reiner have a visitor? No visitations were scheduled, though on rare occasions they occurred without notice. It remained outside the room and listened.

"Why? Why me?" It sounded not so much a question as a tearful plea. "I don't understand. Why, God? Why?"

It heard no other voices and determined she was simply talking to herself, as many isolated patient-residents were inclined to do. It entered, carrying its hygienic provisions, and moved to the bed's right side.

"Good afternoon, Ellen. How are you today?"

She didn't reply; instead, she fumbled to take hold of a tissue, which she used to clear her nasal passages.

"It is time for me to bathe you."

"I don't want to. Go away."

"You know you must be cleaned. I can take you to the shower room or I can do it here."

"I don't want you to. I don't want you to touch me."

It searched its databanks for the proper situational response. "I do not understand your reluctance, Ellen. I know your previous caregiver bathed you at the proper intervals."

She turned away from him. "I don't want you to see me. My body's so … it's so …"

"Your previous caregiver saw your body many times. I fail to comprehend your—"

"It's different. You're different. He was like a machine. You're …"

"I am also a machine, Ellen. I am an automated caregiver."

She didn't respond.

"I promise to be gentle. Let me remove the bed coverings."

She acquiesced, although she kept her face turned away.

It took a moment to evaluate its observations. Situations in which the patient-resident was uncomfortable could often be mitigated by conversation. So it accessed its creative response program. In doing so, it conducted a visual search of the room, marking the photographic representations above the bed.

"Is that you in the photographs, Ellen?" it asked, pulling the shift up above her waist and beginning to wipe her clean.

"Yeah," she said, her face still turned away, staring at bare wall. "That was me."

"It appears you were a performer of some kind."

"Dancer—I was a dancer," she said irritably. "Not that you'd ever know it by looking at me now."

"That is very interesting. How did you become a dancer?"

"I just liked to dance, that's all."

"In the black and white photograph, the one where you are surrounded by other dancers, you look very young."

Ellen turned her face, angling to look up at the photo. "That's when I was on *American Bandstand*, an old TV show. I was just a kid."

"Were you a professional dancer?"

"Later I was—when I moved to New York." She chuckled at some private recollection. "For a time I was what they called a 'go-go dancer.' I worked at some real dives to put myself through dance school. Places like *Rocky's* and *The Gull's Inn* ... those were the days."

It observed the conversation was indeed distracting her from its ministrations, so it pursued the topic.

"I did not realize they had schools for dancing."

"Sure they do. I studied for a long time with Hanya Holm. Talk about an old biddy. After that, I joined Erick Hawkins' Modern Dance Company. We traveled all over. Of course, that was before my first marriage—before I had my son." For a moment she looked wistful, as if sorting through fond memories. "I didn't dance anymore after Edward was born. At least not professionally."

"How many children do you have?"

"Just the one. I've got a grandson now, and two *great* grandkids—can you believe it?"

"Certainly."

"That's their picture over there, with their father and mother."

"They appear to be very healthy," it said, not certain how to respond.

It tended to a few final details and pulled down her shift. "I am finished now, Ellen. Do you require anything before I go?"

"No."

"All right. I will check on you later."

She turned her face away again.

It couldn't tell if she was looking at the photos on the wall or if she'd closed her eyes.

"Happy Thanksgiving, Ellen."

"Hmmph. What have I got to be thankful for? You tell me, Owen."

Patient-resident Ellen Reiner had addressed it as "Owen" for such an extended period that it had begun to think of itself in that manner.

"I understand your Thanksgiving meal will be a special treat," Owen stated, checking the medic monitor and recording the data output.

"Not likely. The food in this place tastes like mush. It's no wonder, seeing as how it's made by tasteless machines."

"It is true the automated kitchen workers have no sense of taste, but I am certain they prepare your meals to the exact dietary specifications provided."

"Yeah, specifically bland."

"There are currently 5,397 patient-residents quartered within Repository Carehouse 319, and the food must be prepared in a manner to accommodate everyone."

"Yeah, well, a little spice now and then would do them good."

"I have no doubt the sustenance provided complies with all nutritional guidelines, Ellen. If you would like, I can—"

"Piss on nutrition! I want something that's sweet or sour or puts a fire in my belly. Hell, I got nothing else to look forward to. You'd think I could get a decent meal every once in a while."

Owen straightened the bed coverings, tucking in the length where necessary, and removed the bag from the bedside commode.

Ellen reached across the bed and fumbled with something.

"I can't work the remote anymore," she said with exasperation. "My damn hands are too deformed. There's an old movie I wanted to watch, but I can't change the channel."

"I can do that for you. What channel would you like me to select?"

"It's *Singing in the Rain* with Gene Kelly. I think it's channel 98."

Owen activated the channel selector. "Is this correct?"

"Yeah, that's it. Oh, it's already half over."

She stared at the screen for some time as Owen completed its duties, and then spoke as if her attention were elsewhere. "I've had some great Thanksgiving dinners, you know. Garlic mashed potatoes, stuffing made with celery and onion and pine nuts, golden brown turkey—cooked just right so it was still moist, you understand—candied yams, cranberry sauce. ... " Her voice trailed off as if she were still reminiscing but not verbalizing.

"Can I get you anything, Ellen?"

"No." Then, reconsidering, she gestured toward the remote with her gnarled fingers and said, "You could turn the volume up for me."

Owen complied. On the video screen, as the title suggested, a man was singing and dancing through a rainstorm. Despite the meteorological situation and his saturated condition, he was smiling. Nothing in Owen's programming derived any logic from it. It was the way humans were.

"I will go and let you watch your movie now."

It was on its way out when it heard Ellen say softly, "Thanks, Owen."

Owen's internal alarm sounded. The medic monitor in room 1928 was summoning it: it must disregard normal routine and check on the patient-resident's condition immediately.

Upon entering the room, it initially failed to locate patient-resident Ellen Reiner. It did, however, note the medic monitor was emitting its warning *beep* and recognized the patient-resident's vital signs were fluctuating dangerously. It activated its exigency video record option and located the patient-resident on the floor next to the bed. Owen bent down next to her.

"Ellen, what happened?"

"I was trying, uhh … to see out the window," she said weakly.

Owen evaluated her response and reactions. She was apparently in a tremendous amount of pain. "Damn legs don't work anymore. They just collapsed right out from under me."

"You should have called for me to help you."

"I didn't want to … bother you."

"Regardless, that window is too high for you. Do you not remember?"

"I guess I forgot."

"Do not be alarmed; I have alerted an emergency medical team. They will be here momentarily."

"No!" she exclaimed so vehemently her body convulsed and she gasped in obvious pain. "I don't want them," she managed to whisper. "I don't want to be saved. Just let me go. Let me be done with it."

Owen was trying to formulate an appropriate response when the EMT, consisting of two humans and an automated assistant, rushed in. Owen moved aside as they took their places around the patient-resident. She began crying as soon as she saw them.

"No," she wept, "no, no."

Owen stood there, its ceramic ocular arrays focused intently on patient-resident Ellen Reiner. There was nothing it could do. It wasn't programmed for medical emergency procedures.

"Looks like a broken hip," one of the humans said. "Blood pressure's dropping dangerously low. We've got to get her to surgery."

The automated assistant distended the compact gurney it carried, and they transferred Ellen onto it as gently as they could. Still she cried out—whether in pain or protest, Owen could not be certain. All it could do was watch as they pushed her out, and listen as her tearful cries down the corridor.

When its audio receptors could no longer discern her voice, it replayed the incident video. Had it failed somehow in its duties? Could it have acted differently to prevent the injury from occurring? It listened to her words, then listened again … trying to understand.

"I don't want them. I don't want to be saved. Just let me go. Let me be done with it."

It didn't matter how many times Owen replayed the recording, or how it attempted to dissect the phraseology, it still didn't comprehend.

Three weeks and two days had passed since Owen had last gone into room 1928. There had been no reason to. Then it received notification that patient-resident Ellen Reiner had been returned to her room. It found the notification to be welcome and accompanied by an indefinable inclination to care for her once again. However, upon seeing Owen, Ellen acted less than pleased. Her reaction was, it seemed, more akin to acrimony.

"I am glad to see you have returned, Ellen. I hope your stay in the hospital facility was pleasant."

She failed to respond, so Owen went about its duties but continued its attempts to engage her.

"I understand you are still recovering from your injuries and must not attempt to stand or walk again. Please inform me if you need to get out of bed, and I will provide a wheelchair."

There was still no response, and Owen discovered her silence to be a source of agitation it could not define or locate within its systems.

"It will be Christmas soon. I am pleased you were able to return before the holiday. I understand members of your family will be visiting on the 24th of the month. I am certain you look forward to that."

More silence. Then, as Owen attempted to formulate a new line of conversation, Ellen spoke up, her tone harsh and unforgiving.

"Why didn't you just let me die?"

"What do you mean, Ellen?"

"You heard me. Why didn't you let me die? I asked you to. I begged you."

"You are in my charge, Ellen. I am programmed to care for you. I cannot do anything to harm you."

"Nobody asked you to. I just asked you to leave me alone—let me be."

"Not calling for medical assistance when you were so seriously injured would be the equivalent of harming you, Ellen."

Her eyes bore into Owen with what it determined was an angry stare. A dewy film glazed over them, and her tone altered. It was more pleading than demanding, and several times the cadence of her voice broke with emotion.

"You should have let me die, Owen. That's what I wanted. I'm not really alive anyway. What kind of life is this? I'm just waiting around … waiting to die. That's all anyone in this place is doing. This is just death's waiting room, don't you know that?"

She sobbed once and then seemed to physically gather herself, reining in her emotions.

"Hell, they shoot horses don't they?"

"Shoot horses?"

"Animals—they treat animals more humanely than they do people."

Owen didn't respond. It was occupied, trying to comprehend what she had said. The word "humanely" was not incorporated into its vocabulary, but its root contained the word *human*. Did it mean to be treated as a human? If so, why would horses be treated more human than humans?

"It's the bureaucrats and the moralists. That's who's keeping me alive. Them and those who own this *carehouse*—who own *you*, Owen. All they really care about is collecting their compensation. I'm just a source of income—a husk defined by profit motive. They've taken the choice away from me. But it's my choice," she said, pockets of moisture now evident under her eyes, "not theirs."

Ceasing its work, Owen stood listening, trying to reconcile its programming with what she was saying.

"I am sorry, Ellen. I am sorry you are so unhappy."

"It's not your fault, Owen. It's not your fault."

Despite her words, Owen detected an irregularity in its systems that might indicate a fault. It would need to perform a self-diagnostic before continuing with its duties.

Owen didn't realize Ellen's visitors had arrived until it had already walked in on them.

"I am sorry, Ellen," it said, stopping short. "I was unaware your guests had arrived. I will come back later."

"No, it's okay, Owen. Stay. Do what you need to do. They don't care."

"Gee, Great Grandma, is that your robot?" asked the older of the two young boys standing next to her bed.

"That's Owen. He takes care of me. He's a … what are you again, Owen?"

"An automated caregiver."

"Yeah, right." She turned to the other side of her bed to address the man standing there. "So where's Alisha?"

"You know, it being Christmas Eve and all … she had a lot to do."

"Is that right?" Ellen replied caustically.

"Well, you know how this place upsets her so, Grandma."

"It doesn't exactly make me feel like a princess."

Her grandson shifted his feet uncomfortably, looking at a loss for words.

"I hope you like the cookies we made for you, Great Grandma," the older boy said.

"I'm sure I will, Matthew."

"Well, we'd better go now and let your great grandma rest. Give her a hug goodbye and wish her a merry Christmas."

The older boy reached over and hugged her. "Merry Christmas, Great Grandma."

The younger boy kept his hands at his sides and edged back a few inches.

"Go on, Todd, hug your great grandma."

"He's scared of me," Ellen said. "Don't force him. It's all right. Great Grandma Ellen isn't a very pretty sight these days."

Her grandson bent down and kissed her forehead. "Merry Christmas, Grandma. I wish … I wish I could—"

"Get along now," she said sharply, cutting him off. "Santa will be here soon, and these boys need to get to bed so they don't miss out."

"Okay, boys, wave goodbye to your great grandma."

The older boy waved and said, "Goodbye, Great Grandma." The younger one hesitated, waved quickly in her direction, and then hurried to catch up with his father and brother.

When they were gone, Owen spoke up. "It must be nice to have family members come and visit. Will your son be coming too?"

"My son died a long time ago. Car accident."

Owen picked up her dinner tray and swept a few loose crumbs onto it. "Well then, it was nice that your grandson could visit."

"I'd just as soon he didn't. I feel like a hunk of scrap metal weighing him down. I don't like being a burden."

"You are not a burden, Ellen."

"Maybe not to you, Owen, but to family … well, I guess you wouldn't understand that."

"No, Ellen, I would not understand that."

"Owen, is that you?"

Sounding only partially awake, Ellen rolled over and opened her eyes.

"Yes, Ellen."

"I was just lying here, listening to the rain. Can you hear it?"

"Yes, I can. Would you like me to turn on the sound screen so it does not bother you?"

"No, no … I like listening to it. It's soothing, don't you think?"

"Soothing? I do not know what soothing is, Ellen."

"I've always liked the sound of rain. I don't know why exactly—I just do."

"They are holding Easter Sunday services in the community room this morning. Would you like to attend? I have brought your wheelchair."

"Is it Easter already?"

"Yes, it is. Would you like to join the worshipers?"

"To worship what? God? God deserted me a long time ago. He's not getting any more from me."

"I am sorry. My records must be incorrect. Your file designates you as a Christian of the Lutheran denomination. Accordingly, I thought you might wish to take part in the ritual."

"I *am* a Christian—was my whole life. I believed, I had faith, I worshiped God—then He did this to me. Do you think I should worship Him for this?" She held up a twisted, disfigured hand, but could only extend her arm a few inches from her body. "Do you think my faith should be stronger because He turned me into this *thing*?"

"I cannot say, Ellen. I am not programmed to respond to philosophical questions concerning faith or religion. I do not comprehend the concepts involved."

"There was a time I would have pitied you for that, Owen. I would even have thought less of you."

Owen waited to see what else Ellen would say, but the only sound was the patter of rain against the window.

"All right, Ellen. I will return your wheelchair to the storage unit."

"Yeah, take it back, Owen. I don't need it. What I have to say to God I can say right here."

Inside the staff maintenance bay, surrounded by several other diligent caregivers, Owen completed its routine self-diagnostic and filed its monthly patient-resident assessments. It didn't speak to any of its co-workers. That only occurred when its duties required such interaction. Its programming necessitated only that it converse with the patient-residents under its charge, and even then, only with those who were coherent enough to carry on conversations. So, as it exited the maintenance bay, Owen didn't acknowledge any of its peers. It simply traversed the familiar corridor, crossed the homogeneous tile mosaic, and began its evening duty cycle.

Then, a notion occurred to it. It was an unusual notion, though not inordinate. It would break from routine. Instead of beginning with the nearest cubicle, it would go first to room 1928, to see Ellen.

It discovered her dinner tray was still full. Except for some minor spillage, the meal appeared to be untouched. Ellen ignored Owen's presence, seemingly intent on the video screen.

"Ellen, why have you not eaten any of your dinner? Are you not feeling well?"

"It's crap! It all tastes like crap. Take it away—I don't want it."

"You must eat, Ellen. If you refuse to eat, I must nourish you intravenously. I know you would not like that."

"You're damn right I wouldn't."

"Please, then, try to eat some of your dinner."

"I can't! I can't, okay? My hands don't work anymore," she

blurted out, her distress evident in the cracking of her voice. "Look at them. Look at how deformed they are. I can't even pick up a spoon anymore. I'm helpless. I'm useless. I can't even feed myself."

Owen could see she was angry and struggling to hold back the tears welling up in her eyes.

"You should have called me, Ellen." The automated caregiver moved the swivel table aside and sat on the edge of the bed. "I can feed you."

"I don't want you to. I don't want you to feed me like I'm some kind of baby."

"Why not, Ellen? That is why I am here. I am here to care for you, to do what you cannot. That is my function." Owen took the spoon and scooped up a small bite of pureed vegetables. "Please, let me help you."

Owen held the spoon out, but Ellen remained steadfast, refusing to open her mouth. Owen, too, didn't move. Displaying the patience of its programming, the indefatigable property of its metallurgy, it held the spoon until Ellen relented and took it into her mouth. She swallowed the morsel as Owen cut into the portion of soy burger. With some reluctance, she took a second mouthful. It waited as she swallowed, then offered her a third spoonful. She wavered momentarily, looking up at Owen.

"It still tastes like crap, you know."

Owen waited outside Ellen's room as a facility doctor conducted the required biannual examination. Ellen had been pleading with the doctor for several minutes, and had begun to cry. The sound elicited a response in Owen. It was an impulse to hurry to her side—to care for her. However, Owen determined such action would be inappropriate and held its position.

"Please," it heard her beg, "please give me something. Help me."

"Now, Ms. Reiner, everything's going to be all right. You're going to be fine," the doctor responded, though the accent affecting his pronunciation made him difficult to comprehend. "Don't worry now. You're not going to die."

"You're not listening to me. I *want* to die. I don't want to live like this."

"Now, now. Of course you don't want to die. You shouldn't say such a thing. You're going to live a long time. Everything's going to be all right. I'll give your caregiver the prescription for the anti-itch lotion, and then I want you to have a nice day. All right?"

The doctor passed Owen as if it weren't there, making no attempt to input Ellen's aforementioned prescription. Owen decided the doctor would likely file all the appropriate prescriptions when he had completed his examinations, so it stepped in to check on Ellen.

As soon as she saw Owen, she made a concerted effort to halt her tears and wipe away any evidence that she'd been crying. So Owen checked the medic monitor, giving her a moment to compose herself.

"It's so hot, Owen. I can't get this sheet off. Could you help me?"

"Certainly, Ellen. Would you like it pulled all the way down?"

"Yes."

"I am sorry the temperature is uncomfortable for you. The climate controls are not functioning properly, but a repair crew has been notified."

"It's so hot for June. It must be at least 80 outside."

"The date is August 9th, Ellen."

"It's August already?"

"At last report, the exterior temperature was 92 degrees Fahrenheit."

"August?" she mumbled to herself. "What happened to July?"

"If there is nothing else you need, I will tend to my other patient-residents now."

Owen turned to leave.

"Don't go!" Ellen called out. She hesitated, then said with less despair, "Please don't go yet. Stay with me for a while."

Owen contemplated the unusual request. Its atypical nature, coming as it did from patient-resident Ellen Reiner, required further consideration. However, its schedule necessitated it see to its other patient-residents' needs. It began calculating the time necessary for it to complete its shift responsibilities, then abruptly ceased its computations.

"All right, Ellen. I will stay a while longer."

"Oh, Owen, it's so nice to be outside. You don't know."

The automated caregiver carefully maneuvered the wheelchair down the narrow cement pathway. A carpet of lush green grass extended away on both sides, and a stand of oak trees was several yards away. It was a clear day. The sun was high above, and the sky was bright blue.

The impromptu excursion outside the repository, though not unprecedented, required Owen to circumvent protocol. It was not wholly at ease with its actions, but found justification in the form of Ellen's emotional transformation.

"I am glad you are enjoying it, Ellen. When I learned about this location so near the facility, I concluded you might appreciate a brief outing."

"But not too brief, okay?"

"We will stay as long as we are able. I will have to return to my other duties soon."

"This isn't a day for duties, Owen. This is a day to feel the warmth of the sun on your skin, to admire the color of the autumn leaves, and smell the flowers."

"I am not equipped with olfactory senses, Ellen."

"Too bad. But you can see, and you can feel the sun, can't you?"

"I do sense the heat on my exterior overlay."

"Oh look! Look there! It's a little stream. Can we go down there by the water? Please, Owen."

"I will attempt to move you closer."

It gently pushed the wheelchair off the path and across the grass to a spot near the tiny waterway. It locked the chair's wheels and stood patiently by.

"I could sit here all day. It's so beautiful. Listen to the sound the water makes as it rushes by. Don't you wonder where it's going?"

"The question of its ultimate destination did not occur to me, Ellen. However, I could research the geography of the area if you would like."

"No, no, it's just the *idea* of imagining where it's going." She looked up at Owen, but there was no expression to decipher on its artificial face. "I'm sorry, Owen. I forgot for a second. You probably think this is all so silly."

"I do not believe it is silly if it pleases you, Ellen."

"It does, Owen. It does. Look! Over there—it's a butterfly. Isn't it beautiful?"

Though it understood the word, beauty as a concept was beyond its programming, so Owen didn't reply. It stood impassively with its charge, watching the insect's flight.

Neither spoke for some time, nevertheless, Owen could tell Ellen's disposition had improved by a degree that was quantifiable. That generated within its systems the concept of a task adequately performed, a vague notion it could only define as fulfillment.

"I must return you to your room and resume my other duties now, Ellen."

"So soon?"

"I do have other patient-residents I must attend to."

"I understand."

Owen unlocked the wheels and turned the chair.

"Owen?"

"Yes, Ellen?"

"Thank you."

"You are welcome, Ellen."

The corridors of Repository Carehouse 319 were filled with the distant, muted sounds of revelry. So many patient-residents had tuned their video screens to the same programming that the festive broadcast echoed stereophonically throughout the facility. Owen understood it was the celebration of a new year—a new calendar decade.

The occasion seemed to call for much noise and frenetic activity, but it still had its duties to perform. Its patient-residents still had to be cared for. Soiled sheets still had to be changed, meal trays cleared, waste receptacles emptied. It began, as called for according to its self-revised routine, by checking on room 1928.

Ellen lay on her side, facing away from the entry. Unlike most of those in the facility, her video screen was inactive.

"Ellen, do you not want to watch the New Year's festivities?"

When she failed to respond, Owen moved closer. Her eyes were open, but there was no sign of recognition in them.

"Ellen? Are you all right?"

Her eyes tilted upward, but she didn't move.

"I can barely hear you," she said. "I think I'm losing my hearing."

Owen adjusted its audio output. "Can you hear this?"

She nodded.

"Everyone is watching the New Year's Eve broadcast. Would you like me to activate your screen?"

She shook her head curtly and looked away. It was apparent to Owen that Ellen was not behaving normally. Her disposition displayed symptoms analogous to severe depression. Nevertheless, before resorting to a petition for psychological counseling, Owen resolved to draw her into conversation.

"It is unfortunate your family members were not able to visit you for the Christmas holiday this year. However, it was thoughtful of them to send that splendid videocard. I conjecture they will schedule a visit soon. Do you agree?" She didn't respond, so Owen continued, "If you do not wish to watch the celebration here in your room, I can bring a wheelchair and escort you to the community room. It is my understanding there is an ongoing party to celebrate the coming year. Would you like that?"

Her head moved sluggishly side-to-side.

"Please leave me alone, Owen. I just want to be left alone."

"All right, Ellen. I will leave you. However, I will return later. Perhaps you can instruct me in that card game you described."

Owen waited for a reply, for some acknowledgment, but there was none. So it left her as she requested.

Owen's internal alarm sounded, and it noted with unaccustomed distress that the alert originated with the medic monitor in room 1928. It hurried to the room, confirming the danger with the *beeping* medic monitor upon arrival. It was about to initiate the video record option but discontinued. Ellen was in her bed, eyes open and apparently fine though her breathing was labored. Owen went to her.

"Ellen, can you hear me?"

"Yes, but … but it's hard to breathe."

"Here, use this." It detached the oxygen mask from its niche in the wall and placed it over her face. "Your blood pressure is diminishing. I am going to alert the emergency medical team."

With the mask over her face she couldn't respond, but she reached out as best she could and rested her gnarled fingers on Owen's inorganic arm. Her motivation wasn't clear, yet somehow, Owen felt it understood the meaning of her touch.

"If you do not receive immediate medical attention, you will likely suffer heart failure. I am required to summon assistance."

Owen thought it discerned a slight sideways movement of her head, as if she were attempting a negative response. Her eyes implored, probing inexplicably into Owen's systems, forcing it to reconcile the needs and desires of its patient-resident with its overriding program.

Ellen brushed aside the mask with the back of her crippled hand and tried to speak, but all Owen heard was a gasp for air. It reached down, placed its distal extremity reassuringly on her forehead, and left it there until her eyelids gave way and fell.

Owen checked the medic monitor, looked back at Ellen for a protracted moment, and then stepped away from the bed. It deactivated the monitor and exited the room to resume its duties.

It wasn't supposed to be here—it was scheduled to perform a self-diagnostic. However, it had concluded that bypassing routine on this singular occasion would not be detrimental to its overall performance. Instead, it had chosen to exit Repository Carehouse 319 and retreat to a particular grassy mound, where it could feel the sun's warmth on its exterior overlay, contemplate stored memories, and listen to the water as it rushed by on its way to destinations unknown.

Breakers

By James C. Bassett

It's a dangerous life, breaking is. Months at a time in deep space, living in a cramped ship with nothing to do—or living in your suit for days or even weeks at a time when there is work. Dangerous, dirty, backbreaking work. Always dreaming of the one Big Score that will let you retire. Not many ever hit it … but then, not many breakers ever live to retire anyway.

Shipbreaking can be deadly in drydock, even on the lunar surface. Us freelance crews do it in the hard deep—if a torch slips, a jagged edge clips your suit, or even a micrometeorite wings into you, that's the end of your run. No big rescue ops out here: medical is limited to whatever's on hand and whatever the rest of your crew knows how to do. Some of the engines of the ships we're salvaging are hot and dirty as well … and sometimes not just the engines, either.

I'm actually something of a legend for my longevity—nine years without even a close call. And don't call it luck, either. Breakers don't believe in luck … at least, not the ones who survive. Start thinking there might be such a thing as luck, something beyond your control, and you start getting careless. Nothing kills you faster than being careless. Breaking ships is dangerous enough without leaving anything to chance—anything at all.

So, we don't believe in luck … but we do believe in opportunity. We were limping our way back to Chang'e Station after two months out, and we picked up a cargo ship heading almost straight for us—so we jumped at it. We were running low on everything from food to fuel to patience, but our hold and our racks were empty, all our tow cables furled—we'd had three unsuccessful runs in a row, two wrecks not being worth the work and the Shrike Nine beating us to the third by less than a day. If we didn't snap at this bone, we'd have to reach deep down into the ship's common fund to resupply.

A quick check showed that there were no other crews in striking distance this time. The ship was all ours—if we could catch it.

For us freelancers, catching ships in the deep is the key to our salvage rights, key to our survival. There's not many ships that are worth the owners paying someone to break. Drydock fees are criminal, and the backlog runs about two years so drydock work is almost always on new ships, not salvage. Some owners down their ships on Luna or Mars, but even then, the cost of official labor, with all the safety regs and government interference, usually outstrips the salvage value. And of course it's only the official breakers who keep up with all their payments—official and not—who can make use of the facilities and infrastructure. Even if there were a way around the unions, surfacing a ship also brings environmental and safety fines for the "accident" that make almost any salvage unprofitable for owners.

Thanks to all that, it's almost always cheaper to just abandon a ship. But, leaving a dead ship in the spaceways comes with even bigger fines. So, most ships get boosted out of the ecliptic and aimed toward the sun.

We can't afford to burn fuel across the solar system to reach a ship, so unless two crews happen to be in the same region when a ship is abandoned—as happened with us and the Shrike Nine— whoever is closest usually gets the salvage uncontested. It makes for less real competition, but also a shorter timeline. If you don't want to spend three years slingshotting back home (and trust me, you don't), you've got to burn fuel—and money—to boost out of the gravity well and get back directly. The longer we spend chasing and working a ship, the closer to Sol we get, and the more reaction mass it takes to return home. Wait too long to vacate, and you spend more on fuel than you make from the salvage. Or worse, *you* end up as salvage.

This ship was going to be a real trick. We had her to ourselves, but she hadn't simply been abandoned—whoever had ditched this ship had turned it toward Sol at top speed. That was damned suspicious—even if an owner doesn't pull off the remaining fuel when they evacuate their personnel, there's absolutely no reason to burn it all off before the ship vaporizes—but we were finally in the right place at the right time, and we couldn't afford to pass it up.

We weren't expecting much. She was just a cargo ship, after all—not much different from our own Terrapin (the name a joke, based on the ungainly appearance of what is essentially a giant cargo hold with engines bolted on). You can always salvage the engine cores, though, if nothing else. Even if they're not reactive enough to power another spaceship, they'll still be plenty hot to run a home or a small flier. Then you've got adaptive electronics, precious metals, life support and safety systems. ... And this ship obviously still had some fuel left, which our own dangerously low tanks were desperate to swallow.

It took a good bit of what we had left to catch her. We were almost there when Saburo casually said, "Company on the way."

We all glanced at one another. Fights between breakers are almost unheard of, but it's that "almost" that's the trouble. I know of three and they all ended badly. Very badly. A battle in the deep isn't like what they show in action vids. There's no laser beams and glittering explosions—there's just a deadly game of chicken, two ships nudging together, trying to cause more damage to the other than they take themselves. And then ... breakers fight dirty, and even a clean fight in space is nasty business. It's hand-to-hand in suits and microgravity, and it's all or nothing—you win or you die. Sometimes everybody dies. Usually. The fights I know of, there were only five survivors and only two of them survived long enough to be rescued. They were both executed for piracy and murder.

So I asked, "When does the party start, Cap'n?"

"Hard to say. It's just a blip near Ceres right now. Not enough telemetry yet. Two weeks, maybe?"

Everyone looked around again, and burst into laughter.

"Two weeks?" Romy said, disbelieving. "We'll be done by then!"

"Why would they even waste the fuel?" Parson asked.

Jokes and laughter continued as we came abeam and started our visual, but I stayed quiet. There was definitely something funny about the situation, but not the kind of funny that calls for laughter. There was no reason for another crew to be heading our way. No *good* reason.

If there was any good news, it was that our salvage seemed to be in perfect condition—as close to brand new as I've ever seen a ship. By the time we were ready to grapple on, Gillie had traced the registration and we knew everything there was to know about her—which was basically nothing.

She was unnamed and registered to a small shipping company owned by an empty holding company called Arkadian Enterprises. Beyond that, she was a black hole. No crew manifests, no cargo records, no dockage reports. The ship appeared not to have carried any cargo—or to have done anything at all. That explained why she looked so new, and why other breakers were so interested.

Suddenly, this wasn't looking like a salvage run anymore. If we could tow the ship back and sell her whole—well, it was looking like we might have made our Big Score. What still made no sense was why the ship had been abandoned in the first place … but we could worry about that after we finished counting our money.

Saburo updated telemetry and then the laughter stopped:

"Revised ETA: thirty-seven hours."

"What?"

"They're coming in hot," Saburo explained.

"Obviously," Dunny said. "But why?"

Something else troubled me more. "And how? What crew has engines like that?"

"Maybe they kept some toys from their last salvage."

It still made no sense, unless our rivals knew more about this ship than we did. If the stakes really were that high, they might be a lot more willing to risk a fight—but if the stakes really were that high, then so were we.

"What could they know?" Gillie asked. "I had to dig just to find the registration. There's sure as hell nothing public about this ship."

"Then let's make it public," I suggested.

Saburo eyed me. "What do you mean?"

"If the media think there's any chance at all of a fight, you know damn well there'll be half a hundred scopes on us—and on them. If they so much as scratch our paint, they won't be able to port anywhere in the solar system without being arrested for piracy."

Sure enough, by the time I was cycling the lock for EVA, our rivals had slowed to a less suspicious, less aggressive speed ... but they kept coming.

Our first priority was to flip-and-brake, slowing the headlong rush toward the sun. Even if this did just end up as another salvage mission, the farther we could stay from old Sol and his gravity well, the easier—and cheaper—it would be to get back home.

While we were taking care of that, a quick check determined that there was enough reaction mass to get the ship back to Luna— if she was worth the effort. So while everyone else worked on slowing us down, I took Romy and set off exploring. The crew module looked like any other on a cargo transport—like a newer, nicer version of our own. The surprise came when I floated into the hold.

Whether you carry fuel, chemicals, raw materials, or—like us—pieces of broken ships, all holds look alike. A girderwork shell skinned over with spun carbon maximizes the usable volume and minimizes any internal obstructions that could interfere with loading and storage. Basically, a hold should be as hollow as possible.

Not this one. I expected to see half a million cubic meters of nothing when I opened the access hatch. What I saw was a hallway.

A hatch at the other end led to a small room lined with closets full of isosuits. A side door led to a washroom with actual showers—pressure sprayers, suction drains, actual *water*.

Someone had spent a *lot* of money retrofitting a brand new cargo ship, only to abandon it. I couldn't help but wonder why even while I was busy trying to refigure the trade value of our salvage. The more that number grew, the more suspicious I became.

The next room was big—very big, but still just a small fraction of the sum. It looked like it had been a workshop or something, but only the benches remained. Whatever equipment had once been there was gone.

I wandered the maze for half an hour, making a mental catalog of all the nothing I found. Lots of similar workshops, all stripped bare. Living quarters—nice ones—for dozens of crew members or workers meant there would be extra life systems, which would bring high salvage if they hadn't been removed.

I finally came to a corridor with a large security door at the far end. With the ship's power out, the manual failsafe would be engaged, so I popped the access panel and spun the wheel, and floated into the biggest chamber I had found yet. My heads-up told me it was at the center of the hold. There was a lot of junk in there—by the looks of it, nothing valuable, just random junk that hadn't been worth hauling away, although someone had still gone to the trouble of moving it all and locking it up in here.

A score of heavy doors ran the length of one wall. I opened the one nearest me.

If I'd been dirtside, I would have fallen down. Even there in microgravity, with my boots gripping the deck, my knees went all wobbly and I swayed like a wildflower in a spring breeze.

The comm slapped me back to my senses. "We're being scanned," Saburo said.

"Scanned?" Keno asked. "What the hell do you mean, scanned?"

"We're picking up pulses from those other breakers. They're trying to read us."

"No," Gillie protested, disbelief dripping in his voice. "There's no breakers out there with that kind of equipment."

"Unless they salvaged it."

"What breakers would keep that? We got no use for anything like that—any crew that salvaged a scanner array would sell it in a heartbeat."

I finally managed to jumpstart my brain. "Those aren't breakers out there," I said.

"No?" Saburo asked. "Then who are they?"

"Someone who doesn't want us to find what I just found."

"Yeah? And what did you just find?"

Twenty minutes later, the whole crew had suited up and joined me. Saburo kept the helm but he was watching through our eyes. Everybody could have done the same, of course—but of course, everybody wanted to see it with their own two eyes. Everyone except Parson, that is, who's had just the one since the Delmont salvage went wrong last year.

"Is that what I think it is?" Keno asked.

"Depends on what you think it is," Gillie told him drily.

"And on what it is," Saburo added. "Sluggy, what do you know?"

It was humanoid. After near half an hour staring at it, that was still all I knew for sure. That, and there were sixteen more of them.

When I say it was humanoid, I mean it had four limbs and a head so it looked more like a human than like a starfish. But the limbs were all the same, like a starfish—it wasn't two arms and two legs—and all four limbs had hands. Sort of. Kind of like an orangutan. The head was pretty much human, insofar as it had two things that were probably eyes and something below them that might have been a mouth. Or a mouth and a nose. Or it could just as easily have been an exit.

Speaking of which, that whole area was a complete mystery. If there were genitals, they weren't like any kind I'd ever seen. Everything was covered in a thick girdle-like growth, even tougher-looking than the rest of the skin, or shell, or whatever it was.

Still, something about the thing just seemed too familiar for it to be something *else*. I said, "I don't think it's an alien. I think it's human. Or at least it used to be."

"Then what the hell happened to it? To *them*?"

I shook my head. "Well, that would be the real question, wouldn't it?"

"That ... ," Saburo said, " ... and who did it to them."

In my heads-up, the other ship was still on intercept, moving closer. "Well, I guess we'll find that out in a couple days."

That shut everyone up for a while, until Saburo said, "Okay, everyone back to work. We grab what we can and bug out in 24 hours."

"No, we should leave now," Romy protested, "if they're trying to cover *this* up."

"A ship as fast as theirs, it won't make a difference," I warned.

"That's a point," Saburo said. "If they really want to catch us, they will. And something tells me they will really want to catch us."

"So what do we do?"

Maybe it was because I was senior, or maybe it was because I'd been the one to make the find, but everyone turned to look at me like I had some kind of answer. And maybe I did. If it worked—and if they weren't too trigger-happy.

Saburo sensed it. "Sluggy, what you got?"

It was a good idea, and a better one after some back and forth. We did what we had to do, then headed back to the Terrapin while Saburo took care of the rest of the details. We didn't bother breaking the salvage—if my plan worked, we wouldn't need to. If it didn't, I doubted we'd make it home. Either way, there was no point taking the risk that breaking a ship always brings.

And then we had nothing to do but wait.

Breaking always comes with a lot of down time: waiting to find a ship or boosting toward it or back to base once the salvage is done. Normally, it's just boring—lots of vids and card games and routine maintenance work. I've even known a few breakers who spend their time making sculptures out of scrap—anything at all to pass the days. Not this time.

We were all too tense to do anything. Keno and Gillie came to blows, and Romy and I almost did. It wasn't the wait that got to us—it was waiting *for them*. It was even worse than relying on luck. We were stuck in the position of having to rely on someone else, someone outside the crew. And that's a hell of a lot more unpredictable—and dangerous—than luck.

My plan was a good one; I knew that. It had just one flaw. This other ship, whoever they were— they had to talk to us *before* they blew us into stardust. If they were only interested in shutting us up, nothing would save us … and there wasn't a damn thing we could do except wait and find out which way it was going to go.

Eventually, it was too much for me—the griping, the sniping, the yelling and threats and confrontations over nothing at all—and

I hid myself away from the rest of the crew. You don't survive as a breaker for as long as I have without learning your way around a sickbay, and I had a thing or two to find out.

What I found out didn't surprise me—it was a lot more believable than the alternative—but it did disturb me, and it was a *lot* more disturbing than the alternative. It made me want to hurt whoever was chasing us, and whoever had sent them. It made me want to hurt them all very, very badly.

Fortunately, I got the chance.

The ship finally hailed us as they were heaving to.

"Attention scavenger vessel. You are ordered to cease your illegal operations on a privately registered ship."

Saburo silenced everyone's grumbling with a look, but made his face casual for the camera. "This is registered Salvage Vessel Terrapin," he said evenly. "We found this ship clearly abandoned— crewless, beaconless, well outside established space lanes, and with no registered flight plan. It conforms to all international treaty requirements for establishing salvage rights. Sorry, fellas, but we won her fair."

"Terrapin, prepare to be boarded."

I could see the muscles in his cheeks rope up as he clenched his jaw. "I don't think so."

The comm went dark. We looked around at one another, worried, wondering what was coming next.

The screen lit up again, and the uniform said, "Request a private meeting with your captain."

"This is Acting Captain Saburo Arai. We are a collective crew sharing equal status. What you say to one, you say to us all."

The picture switched to a different uniform, older, with captain's pips at her collar. She did not mask her displeasure nearly as well as Saburo.

"Captain Arai," she said testily, "I will happily meet with

whatever delegation you decide upon—or your entire crew—but it is imperative that I speak to you in private. In person." She inclined her head almost imperceptibly in deference. "On neutral territory, if you wish."

Saburo's mouth didn't so much as twitch, but I could see a smile creeping into his eyes. "Neutral territory? We are in deep space, Captain. There is nothing here but your ship, our ship, and the salvaged property that belongs to us by right of legal taking. However, in order to facilitate this meeting—since you seem reluctant to talk over open broadcast—we will welcome you and your escort aboard the salvaged ship in one hour. Terrapin out."

He broke the link and turned to us with a grim look. "Suit up," he said.

Exactly one hour later, the airlock cycled open and the Captain and her four backups stepped stiffly into the accessway. It had escaped no one's notice that she had identified neither herself nor her ship, and she did neither now.

"Thank you all for meeting with me," she began without preamble. "This is a very delicate situation, I'm sure you're aware, and—"

"Welcome aboard," I broke in. "Before we begin, I just want you to know that you are welcome as well aboard the Terrapin. The airlocks are all greenlit, so no one needs to torch or blow their way in, please. The ship is in bad enough shape already," I added with a defiant grin, "which is why we're so pleased to have obtained this new barge."

"This ship—" Captain Nemo began, but I cut her off again—this was *my* show, not hers.

"I also want to mention that we sent a tightbeam message back to Luna two days ago, after sighting you, and another shortly before radio contact with you. As I'm sure you know."

Her level glare showed not a trace of reaction, which told me I was right.

"Those tightbeams contained sealed files. They have been distributed to several of our representatives. If the Terrapin or any member of its crew experiences any sort of 'accident', those files will be opened and made public. I say this just in case those pistols are only still in their holsters because you wanted to take out our crew members on the Terrapin first so nobody could send any kind of distress call. It occurred to me—to all of us, really— that if someone killed us all and set the Terrapin homeward but something happened halfway there … well, it would be impossible to make a piracy charge stick if the evidence somehow exploded in the deep."

I said it casually, lightly, but the Captain knew better. Her jaw clenched so hard I wondered how she didn't crack any teeth. Other than that, she didn't react, but I saw one of her goon's lips move as he obviously belayed an order to someone.

I hadn't realized just how tense I was until then. With that taken care of—with the plan working and everyone safe—I suddenly felt my body relax so much that the lack of gravity alone kept me upright. I didn't even care if the Captain knew it.

It took me a few more breaths before I trusted myself to speak again. "Now that we all understand one another," I told her, "I'll bet you're just *dying* to know what's in those files."

The Captain already knew that we knew, of course, but she didn't know how much, and I still had a trick up my sleeve.

"It's unsettling, isn't it? Disturbing. Frightening," I said, even though the Captain and her cohort still stood steely-faced and without emotion beyond their visible annoyance at having left us alive.

We were all in that large central chamber, staring at those grotesque bodies. No one had said anything—no one had even moved—for several minutes.

"You will not be permitted to leave here with them," the Captain eventually said, very quietly. She turned to face me and added, "Whatever else happens. I'm telling you this as a simple fact, woman to woman. These specimens are—"

"Oh, you can have them," I told her. "They creep me the hell out. Please, get them off our ship!"

"The ship—"

"The ship is ours. I'm telling *you* this, as a simple fact, woman to woman. It is ours by right of salvage. See, that's what we do, salvage things. You wouldn't believe some of the things we've managed to salvage. For instance, we've got a worlds-class med unit—probably the best of any breakers'. It's beyond overkill for our needs, really, but salvaged medicals can't be certified, so there's no salvage value in them. So we just kept it. You'd really be impressed at what we can do."

The Captain was smart enough to figure I had a point, and she waited for me to make it. She didn't look happy about it, though.

"When we first found these ... things, some of us thought they might be alien," I went on. "But some of us thought they couldn't be—if anybody had actually found aliens, why destroy them? Then again, what else could they be? They sure as hell don't look human."

I pointed to a small mark on the thing in front of me. More than a mark—a nick. "See that? It wasn't easy cutting through that ... shell, carapace, whatever it is. But we took a sample from this *specimen* and ran a genescan."

The Captain's eyes momentarily flashed wide with alarm. I nodded and gave her a smile. "See, I told you you'd be surprised. Dunny was, too—he has to cover a week of my cleaning duty. Turns out these buggers are human after all. And whatever happened to them—whatever was *done to* them—well, it wasn't surgical. These poor bastards were modified genetically."

I faced her square on. "But you already knew that, of course.

And now, so do we. So tell me, what is it? It looks like they've been … adapted … to microgee, to working in the deep without suits. That certainly would make for a cheaper labor force, wouldn't it?"

She didn't say a word, just stared back at me with pure hate.

I waved a glove. "Well, fine, the purpose isn't really important now, I guess. What *is* important—which I know you've already figured out for yourself—is that we didn't just send video in those tightbeams. The first one, sure. But the second contains a full report, including the genescans. I know what you were thinking: video is easy to fake, so you were considering taking your chances with that 'accident'. But a genescan—well, now if anything happens to us, that gets out too. Not just that these are—*were*—human. Those scans are complete—people will be able to match them to records, find out exactly who these folks were. That will make it a lot easier to find out who's responsible for what was done to them … and I'm guessing your bosses wouldn't want that."

Her lips were moving as she turned away from me, but nothing came over the suit-to-suit. I figured she was talking to her ship, probably relaying a message home. It would take 13 or 14 minutes to get there, and the same for a reply. I was pretty certain someone would be standing by—someone important—and that it wouldn't take them long to make a decision, but it was still going to be a long, tense half hour.

A long, tense, *dull* half hour. For about ten minutes, everyone just stood around silently and nothing at all happened. Then the Captain turned to face me again, another challenge.

"There should be seventeen."

"What?"

"There should be seventeen of the specimens. I count only sixteen. Where is the last?"

I shrugged. "This is what we found."

"I will tear your ship apart if I have to—"

"Do whatever you want, Captain, but I'm telling you this is what we found. Even wearing suits, we didn't want to touch them to take the samples—there's no way I'm letting one of those onto the Terrapin. I am *not* riding all the way back to Chang'e with one of them on board. Hell, I don't even like having them *here*, on this ship. Seriously—I *want* you to take them the hell away. We have the genescans—why would we need a body?"

"We will search this vessel," she said.

"You do what you want."

She gave me another killing look, but shut up again. Two of her goons headed out, and the rest of us went back to standing around.

Finally, she informed us, "We will start transferring the specimens to our ship." She looked at me expectantly.

"Hell, no! I told you I'm not getting near them!"

She gave me yet another dirty look but didn't press the issue. We stood by and watched as she and her crew put those things in the isosuits I'd found earlier and moved them out to the airlock. Her two detectives returned eventually, empty-handed, and pitched in. They also double-checked the pile of junk and all the ship's data banks for anything important that might have been missed.

When they were at last ready to go, we opened the airlock and they moved out.

"This vessel is yours," the Captain said icily. "We are clear, are we not, that the continued secrecy of this encounter is the only reason you are leaving here alive?"

I did my best to keep the venom out of my smile as I said sweetly, "Oh, of course."

"Because if even a hint of what you've seen here ever reaches the public, I will personally find each and every one of you and kill you as slowly and painfully as I can."

She turned and jetted off to her own ship without looking back—which was good, because it probably just would have made her more upset if she'd seen me rolling her eyes. At least I hadn't burst out laughing when she turned into Captain Cliché.

They fled. We watched them go until they were just another starpoint, and then returned our attentions to securing our prize for the trip home. There was no need to work during the journey back—the new ship would bring far more whole than broken—so we spent our time one-upping each other with the extravagances we planned with our bounty.

It's been fun, but privately I've begun to think of a future far less outrageous. Retirement—a sprawling house on hectares of land under a soaring and breathable sky. In time, maybe even a family. We've done what every breaker dreams of—we made our Big Score—and I intend to take full advantage of it. After all, if I'm going to change my identity, I might as well change everything else about my life.

We all know we'll have to disappear because the Captain was right—there were seventeen of those things. And we have the missing man.

Once we get back and sell the ship—and the Terrapin—we'll divvy up the common fund and go our separate ways. We'll sell off the ships, and our special salvage goes into special storage—but not for insurance.

The Captain said secrecy was the only thing keeping us alive. But, once we're all new people, the crew of the Terrapin will be dead, essentially. So eventually, when we're all settled into our new lives, we can break the story anyway. We'll sell the news—and the evidence—to the highest bidder, of course.

It's a dangerous life, but that's how breakers always do it.

Inchoate
By Tab Earley

Our first warning was the probe that hurtled through the atmosphere, burning with white heat. We found it in the midst of a crater a mile wide. Pieces of it littered the plain where it landed, shrapnel with scorched skin. We didn't understand what it was, not at first. We didn't understand until the second probe came through the atmosphere—intact, unlike the first. It landed as it was intended to land. It trundled along through the sand on rubber wheels and turned its cameras to take pictures of everything.

We hid from it because we didn't know what it was. If we had known then what was in store for us, we would have destroyed it and all the others that followed … but we didn't know. I can't explain now how we were before. Our minds have been changed—our perceptions have been changed. I just know that we were different then.

More probes came. We couldn't decide if they were intelligent life forms in their own right—we'd never seen anything like them. The technology was far beyond anything we could have or would have created. They rolled around and scooped up samples of soil. They chipped off rock and recorded everything. We didn't understand at the time what they were doing. It took time for our intuitive grasp of the universe to adjust, for us to figure it out. We had been here for thousands of years, perhaps millions. Time had no real meaning for us.

When the first ship prepared to land, we sensed that things were about to change for the worse. We sensed, but we didn't know. We didn't know what they were capable of. We didn't know what we were capable of. There had only ever been us and our understanding of each other. Had we known, we would have interfered and made that first ship ignite in the atmosphere. We would have killed everyone on board, but we would have saved ourselves. I wonder now, though, how many of them we would have had to kill to keep them away.

They buzzed and droned just like their ships did. When the first one stepped out of the ship, some of us wanted to destroy it. Just like a meteor entering the atmosphere, it would have gone up in flames for no apparent reason. We could hear the screams even as we refused to do it. We told ourselves we had no reason to fear while a shadow fell over us. The second ship, the third, and all the others after, blotting out the light as they landed among us.

At the time, we didn't understand what they wanted. The planet was arid, mostly sand and rock. Now we know that they wanted the minerals beneath the sand. They wanted the heavy metals beneath that. I remember the buzzing voice of one of them calling the planet a gold mine. "We're going to be the richest bastards in the galaxy." We didn't understand what it meant. They scorched, gouged, and drilled. The landscape we'd known for an age changed so fast that we hardly recognized it. Where there had been hills and mountains, there were gaping holes in the ground. They filled our canyons with the soil.

Then they came for us. We thought if we hid from them, we would survive. Our planet was hostile to them. They wouldn't stay. They would take what they wanted and leave. But they found us.

Pring rubbed at her eyes and blinked. She looked at the clock on the instrument panel and saw that it was 5 am GMT, Earth time. She'd been studying her subjects for nearly 12 hours with only one break. At least, she was reasonably sure she'd been studying all day—she was losing time lately. For long periods, she found herself staring into space, transfixed, and only when she snapped out of it did she realize that she'd been doing it for an hour, sometimes two hours. It made her wonder what was happening to her mind.

Three weeks ago, the three-person crew of Team Seven had discovered them, buried in the sand of a planet that they had all thought was devoid of life. Alpha 1B was a desert, blasted like Mars. Its surface was sand and stone. The preliminary probes had revealed nothing but some primitive bacteria. No significant life forms. No one could explain why the probes had failed to detect the creatures, or why every instrument also failed to detect them. The technicians had checked and rechecked the systems. There were no faults. Somehow the probes, all sixteen of them, had simply not found the life forms. Pring found that intriguing.

The pennae, as Pring had named them, didn't do much except reproduce. They fed on the planet's bacteria and performed a kind of photosynthesis. They had no limbs, and no discernible heads or tails. There was only a lateral fold on the underside filled with tiny hairs that served for propulsion, such as it was. Pring had discovered the first one, nearly tripped over it, and she'd spent the last three weeks doing intensive research into the creatures and the hidden ecology of Alpha 1B.

W&M Industries, who were funding most of the mission, were more concerned with the minerals that planet Alpha 1B had to offer and less so with a creature that had no obvious commercial value. The International Scientific Coalition, which gave the expedition a veneer of altruism, wanted to know about the creatures' potential use as a food source. A food animal that could live in deserts could potentially adapt to the growing wastelands on Earth.

The problem was that only so many freighters would go between Earth and Alpha 1B, with only so much cargo space. W&M argued that if they didn't find the resources to allow transportation and communication to continue at their present rate, everything on

Earth would grind to a halt—including food production. The Coalition argued that if there was no food to produce, it didn't matter anyway. The situation on Earth was grim—grim enough for Pring to wonder if any of them would make it back and whether there would be anything left if they did.

She looked down at the one she'd been preparing to dissect. It rippled faintly with color, almost iridescent. Pring stared down at it and blinked slowly. It was almost as if there was a pattern. Almost.

"What are you?" she murmured.

She thought she saw a response in the play of colors in its flesh. The creature's skin tones mimicked the movement of sand across the dunes, the play of wind and light from the sun. They even did it indoors, which Pring found odd. Put them together in the large tank that dominated the lab and the undulating patterns of red, purple, and orange spanned the entire group.

She asked the question again, but this time there was no change. She had theorized that the colors were a form of camouflage although, as far as they knew, there was nothing on the planet that preyed on the pennae. There was also the possibility that it was a form of communication similar to the color changes of octopus and squid. Pring didn't know, and she suspected that the Directors didn't care.

There were twenty or so pennae in the tank of varying size, but all the same basic shape. Colors rippled across their collective bodies as if they were one. Pring often found herself watching their collective color movement for long periods of time. It soothed her, like staring at the waves on the sea.

She folded her arms and rested her chin on them, staring into the tank as she did nearly every day. She wondered briefly how many hours she'd lost to it, and shook it off. "And what do we do with you?" she murmured.

"Pring?"

She sat up and turned around. Bev stood in the doorway with an eyebrow raised.

"Pring, are you … talking to them?"

Her face flushed. She'd forgotten the cameras in the ship, and she wondered if Bev had been watching her watch the pennae.

"No, I'm just thinking aloud. It helps me focus my thoughts."

Bev hesitated.

"You've been a little weird lately. You spend more time with these things than with people."

She had nothing to say. Things had been tense within the team for a while now. Nordstrom had been the linchpin in the group, not just the ranking officer but the pillar of their team structure. Now he was gone, and Pring wasn't sure whether Bev was concerned about her teammate or herself.

"I'm finding people a little annoying lately," Pring said. "I know all the Directors care about is the mining, but there's more to this planet than that now."

"You mean the Velveeta Shells and Cheese?" Bev asked.

"I mean the *pennae*. This is an important scientific discovery, and it's being sidelined to make way for the gaping maw of consumption."

"You sound like one of the hippies back on Earth," Bev said. "Look, I know these things are important, but it's not like they're E.T. They're not intelligent, they're not sophisticated—they're not anything, really. You remember how that press conference went where they announced the discovery? No one cared. If they don't sing and dance, they don't matter. I know it's shitty, but that's how people are."

Pring shook her head, her lips drawn into a line. She turned back around and pretended to do something with the control panel in front of her until she heard Bev walk away. She glanced over her shoulder, and then she sank down again to watch the pennae in their tank.

Time passed which might have been minutes and might have been hours. She was determined to figure out just what the purpose of the color patterns was, to nail down a distinct stimulus and reaction connection. She'd performed every test she could imagine and nothing had emerged. So, she simply watched and waited.

Bree poked his head in.

"Captain says you need a break from your pets," he said.

She didn't move but went on looking into the tank. She spoke with her back to him.

"I like that you say 'captain says' as if you're not the captain."

There was a moment of silence, and then she heard him walk up behind her.

"Seriously, you've been in here for three hours. I know they're important, and I know you're angry about what the Directors said. But you've got to relax. If you keep winding yourself up so tight, you'll start imagining the slugs are talking to you."

She sat up and looked sharply at him.

"What's that supposed to mean?"

Bree's demeanor was too much like Bev's, too hesitant and apologetic. It made Pring feel like slamming her fist on the metal table and shaking the instruments.

"Well … you *talk* to them," he said.

Pring sighed.

"I *think aloud*. How many times do I have to say this?"

She didn't mention the lost time to him. There was no need to give him any more reason to worry. They were all on edge already between the mission, losing Nordstrom, and the various demands being placed on them from above.

The inevitable loneliness of being in space for so long, knowing that her only companions were people cherry-picked for their ability to work together, wore on her. There were twenty-four teams scattered over an area the size of Texas. Most still had all four team members. A few, like her own, had lost someone. All the psychological and physical testing in the world could still miss things. So it had been with Nordstrom.

The Coalition had warned them all about the potential for mental disruptions. All four of them had undergone rigorous psychological testing to determine their suitability for space travel and their compatibility with other people in a team. The four of them—Pring, Bree, Bev, and Nordstrom—had been trained together. Each of them had strengths that complemented the others. No massive personality conflicts, no mutinous feelings: just a smoothly-running team that could make it to Alpha 1B and back without killing each other. They had done all their simulations and their training as a team, and by the time they left they shared a close bond.

The problem with the Coalition's surefire team construction was that if the team lost a member, things became unbalanced. The mission could still continue, but the finely-tuned harmony would be off. There was no reason to think that any of the teams would lose a member. All of the pilots, scientists, and technicians were in excellent health, physically fit, and the safety measures for takeoff, space flight, and landing were impeccable. There were fail-safes upon fail-safes. There could be no mistakes.

There *had* been no mistakes, regardless of what Bree and Bev might tell themselves. Nordstrom didn't make mistakes. He had gone into the ventilation shafts claiming that he needed to investigate a minor electrical fault. Nothing important, he had assured her—just a little thing that might become a big thing if he let it go.

"A lot of pieces on this tin can," he said. "You let one shell go, and—shell? Where did that come from?"

He laughed and shook it off. Pring frowned.

"Are you okay, Nordstrom? You don't look so good. Do you have a fever?"

She placed a hand on his forehead, and he rolled his eyes. He took her hand and held it a beat longer than was strictly professional. Her heart thumped, and then he let go.

"I don't have a fever," he said. "Stop worrying."

He gave her a smile over his shoulder and climbed up. She thought about it—maybe he'd just been thinking of the endpoint. Alpha 1B was a desert. Desert, sand, beach, shell: a weird little mental digression, but understandable. The peculiar, off-kilter look in his eyes was just her imagination. Maybe he was stressed; as captain, he pretty much had to be.

When the hatch to the outer hull opened and the alarm sounded, Pring's stomach bottomed out. It wasn't the raw panic of imminent death, just the sudden intuitive knowledge that Nordstrom had not gone to fix a fault. She knew even before they climbed up past the living quarters to the shaft that he was gone. The hatch had closed automatically in response to an unauthorized opening. The hull was secure. There were no leaks, and Pring knew then that there had been no electrical fault.

She couldn't bring herself to check the cameras fore and aft. She didn't need to see Nordstrom's frozen corpse drifting behind them as the ship continued on its pre-programmed course … although she imagined it. Usually at night, as she tried to sleep.

She remembered the moment by the groan Bev let out, by the silent, open-mouthed shock on Bree's face, and the sudden feeling she had that they were all doomed. Moving through a fog, she checked and rechecked the pressure levels, the electrical diagnostics, and hull integrity. Everything was as it should have been. Everything apart from Nordstrom.

Three people could land the rocket. All three of them were

trained as pilots, although none of them had Nordstrom's skill. None of them had his cool-headed command of any situation. In his absence, Bree became captain automatically, although it took him an hour of staring blankly at the control panel before he pulled himself together enough to contact the Coalition and inform them of the accident.

Bree had called it an accident and still did, never mind that getting into the ventilation shafts required Nordstrom to enter a code and unlock a complicated series of bulkheads. Never mind that it required a different set of codes to get through those bulkheads to the hatch that Nordstrom had gone through. A third set of codes was required to open the outer hatch, and it should only have opened if the motion and heat detectors sensed that the body waiting to enter the airlock was in a space suit. Nordstrom had overridden all of those safety features.

Pring thought again about the look on his face before he'd gone up—about the weird verbal misstep he'd made. *Shells.* They had been within sight of the planet, astronomically speaking, but they hadn't landed. They hadn't known about the pennae. They had never even seen them.

It was still hard to believe he was gone. It didn't seem possible that he could have done it so quickly. They had taken their eyes off him because they trusted him—they trusted the testing that had deemed them all fit for travel. Now there were three of them instead of four, as suddenly as if Nordstrom had just blinked out of existence.

Pring couldn't hold back a shudder of revulsion when Archer of Team Fourteen showed her what he'd done. Archer was a go-getter who'd been the minimum age of seventeen when the Coalition teams had followed the probes to Alpha 1B. He was still young, still convinced of his ability to advance within the rigidly stratified hierarchy of the Coalition.

"I didn't want to take any of your specimens," he explained. "I heard you're kind of attached to them, so I went out and got one on my own. They're really hard to find, the big ones. You've gotta admire their camouflage. Anyway, I managed to get one and brought it back to Lab Fourteen to see what I could do with it."

Archer painstakingly explained the way he'd adapted a drill to grind the flesh of the penna into a pulp, which could be fortified with nutrients. Pring pretended to listen and tried to keep her gorge from rising. Her attention was focused on the beaker of pulp in front of her. It no longer resembled a penna in any way except for the grayish hue of the flesh, dead now and absent of any color undulations. It was just meat.

" … there's not much left on Earth to eat, so I thought that given that they can survive in the desert, and given how many of them there are, they'd make a great food source."

She wondered if he had spoken to Bree about that. She somehow managed to swallow, and then spoke. "Possibly," she said. "It doesn't contain much in the way of nutrients, though."

It wasn't much of an argument, and Archer repeated his excited monologue about how they could fortify it with various vitamins. Even given the cost of transport, if they could breed the pennae on earth, such a plentiful source of food would quickly become very cheap. It could feed the whole planet. All Pring had to do was help him write a recommendation that they earmark a portion of the freight capacity for the new foodstuff.

Pring stared at the beaker. She could imagine the pennae being used that way—had already thought of it herself. She had thought about it and discarded the idea. It wasn't just her unnatural attachment to the things, and it wasn't a solid scientific opinion. There was just something about the idea of bringing them to Earth that seemed … unwise. She nursed a growing uneasiness about the pennae that she couldn't attribute to anything concrete. There was nothing about them to suggest danger—nothing poisonous in their chemical make-up, no known defenses except their camouflage—but somehow Pring's fascination had turned to anxiety.

She looked up, blinking. Archer was looking at her expectantly, like a child who'd just done a cartwheel for the first time.

"That's very nice, Archer. Have you sent a report on this to the Coalition?"

He grinned. She pitied his enthusiasm.

"Sure did. I didn't overstep myself, did I? I just wanted to help, you know, solve the food crisis."

Pring nodded. She was revolted and a little upset. It must have been obvious because Archer looked a little disappointed as he took his beaker of flesh with him. He glanced at her over his shoulder, scanned the laboratory full of pennae, and then left.

A month later, two freight ships loaded with pennae of varying size launched, scorching the sand into black glass. Archer went back to Earth with them, along with members of various teams who either wanted to be involved with the process or who simply wanted off Alpha 1B. Eight weeks was a long time to spend in transit to a foreign planet—by the time the first teams had arrived, some of their team members had already applied to return on the first launch back.

Pring had opted to stay. The Coalition had asked her to return so that she could oversee the Earth-bound research into the pennae, but she had declined. Her reasoning was that she needed to do more research *in situ,* and she made clear her apprehensions about bringing the pennae to Earth for any purpose, especially consumption. Naturally, her objections were ignored.

Team Three was one of two teams equipped with a psychiatrist. Although Dr. Barnes's office was exactly the same as Pring's own office in Freighter Seven, down to the furniture, it was distinctly less comfortable somehow. Perhaps it was the familiarity that made it so—the identical layout and furniture, the computer screen on the desk, everything the same apart from the incidental things.

Barnes had a stack of Rorschach cards on her desk. She had ignored Pring's scoffing protests and made her go through them, scribbling notes to herself on a small pad in her cramped handwriting. Pring watched her slender fingers gripping the pencil and half-wished she'd break the lead.

The pencil was one of Barnes's quirks. The Coalition encouraged them all to have little superstitions and rituals—it served as a release for tension and as a way to monitor someone's mental health. Team members who became too reliant on their rituals and totems were watched more carefully. Pring was aware that the time she spent with the pennae had become an official concern.

"Bev tells me your sleep is disrupted," Barnes said in a scrupulously neutral tone. "It's not that unusual, considering the amount of work you've been doing. I have heard from a few little birds that you've been spending an abnormal amount of time in your lab, but that's not surprising given how much there is to learn about these things."

Pring was a scientist, not a psychiatrist, and while she conceded some of the uses of psychology, she still didn't like it. Barnes struck her as a know-it-all, someone who thought she had everyone else figured out.

"According to your team members, you seem to have become withdrawn and often combative. The pennae seem to be a touchy issue. I've read your reports about them and your concerns about introducing them into Earth's ecosystem. Do you feel your concerns are at all … overstated?"

Although Barnes maintained a carefully non-judgmental tone, she couldn't quite mask her condescending skepticism. Perhaps she just wasn't bothering to do so.

"I don't *feel* anything, Dr Barnes. What we have here is an entirely new species, from a planet we previously thought was dead and barren. How this species escaped our initial reconnaissance, we don't know. What effect it will have on Earth's ecosystems, we don't know. What effect it will have on humans if introduced into the food supply, we don't know. There are a lot of very important questions that have yet to be answered, and I think it's damn foolish to proceed as if there are no risks at all."

Barnes folded her hands on her notebook.

"You are aware that crews from Teams Sixteen, Three, Eight, and Eleven have been consuming the processed pennae for some time with no ill effects?"

"Would you like a list of all the things human beings ate until they turned out to cause cancer?" Pring replied. "Doesn't mean it's harmless."

"I concede your point, but I am concerned, Dr. Pring, that your anxieties may be a reflection of personal problems."

By *personal problems* Barnes meant Nordstrom, and Pring was in no mood to discuss that issue. It had occurred to her that she might be losing her mind the same way that he had. However, she didn't feel suicidal or even depressed … what she felt was *afraid*. She didn't know how to explain it to Barnes, and she didn't want to. It would make her sound paranoid and consequently subject to sectioning.

"Personal problems?" Pring asked.

"As I'm sure you're aware, we've been monitoring your team closely since Captain Nordstrom's death."

Pring noticed the way that she said it directly, without euphemism and without any judgment. Clearly, Barnes thought it all had to do with Nordstrom's suicide.

"What do you want me to say? We lost the best member of our team. We're all still recovering from it … but this isn't about Nordstrom."

There was no point in explaining to Barnes the stab of dread she'd felt when the freighter rockets bound for Earth took off. It wasn't just the potential they had to contain some extraterrestrial microbe that could start an epidemic of disease or cause mutations, though she had mentioned that in her reports. It was an older, more primal fear: it was the fear of predation.

It was silly. The pennae were no more a predator than the Earth diatoms they vaguely resembled. They were practically inert— simply dividing and dividing, growing larger or smaller, quietly evolving on their barren planet. There was nothing about them to fear or admire the way that one might fear and admire a shark for being a highly-evolved eating machine. There were no sharks left anyway, not outside of aquariums and museums. There were no predators left at all apart from humans.

"I'm going to ask you a question," Barnes said. "Do you think that your … bond with these creatures is potentially a way to replace the bond you shared with Captain Nordstrom?"

Pring laughed. It felt a little too much like a sob to be comfortable, but it was the only response she could muster. She tried not to think about Nordstrom's verbal slip—it came to her more and more often lately as she felt her own mind unraveling a bit.

"I'm just under a lot of stress," she said. "My scientific opinion is being ignored in favor of commercial interests. I can't be surprised about it, but it does piss me off. Now if you're quite finished poking me, I'd like to go get some rest."

Pring left Freighter Three and went back to her own ship, staring out at the rocky, sandy landscape where she knew thousands upon thousands of pennae were reproducing, growing, and dying. They might have done so for eternity without evolving their simple anatomy. Now no one would know how the pennae might have evolved, because humans had irrevocably changed the planet. They would probably become a new species back on

Earth, adapting to the conditions there and becoming part of the badly damaged ecosystem that she had left behind.

As she walked back to the ship, bouncing gently in the reduced gravity, Pring paused again. The feeling of foreboding she'd been keeping quiet at the back of her mind thrummed and amplified. It was as if the whole planet resonated with it. Something was *wrong*. The warning was there, as broad as the sky. Someone else had to feel it. Someone else had to know.

Bev stood outside the infirmary door and looked through the reinforced glass at the patient inside. The room was quiet now—an unsettled, temporary quiet that would come to an end once the sedatives wore off and the restraints rattled again. The air was still fraught with the noise of argument and escalating insistence. The feeling hung like an emotional echo that bounced from wall to wall.

Bree sidled up beside her. He looked past her into the room at the slight figure in bed. Out of uniform, stripped of the armor of work and her no-nonsense demeanor, Pring looked tiny and fragile … but even in sedation, she looked tense. If there were dreams in her chemically-induced sleep, they weren't pleasant ones.

"How is she?" he asked.

"Same," Bev murmured. "They let the sedatives wear off so that they could talk to her about the delusions, but she wouldn't listen. 'Don't you understand, they're going to kill us all—'"

Bev's voice choked off, and Bree frowned.

"By 'them' she means … she means the pennae, right? She's not convinced there are invisible enemies or anything?"

"Yeah, she means the slugs," Bev said. "I think I could understand fearing an invisible enemy a little more, you know? But being afraid of those things? They're barely alive. I don't get it. They haven't even got *brains*. I think … god, I think she blames those things for Nordstrom's death."

Bree shook his head.

"I don't understand it either," he said. "It may be some latent paranoia coming to the surface, something to do with the Coalition ignoring her objections to the food program. Cassandra complex, maybe."

"Except Cassandra was always right."

She let out a puff of air that was meant to be a laugh, then decided it wasn't funny at all.

We've come to understand you. It has taken longer than we thought, but through our contact with you, we have pierced the opaque veil of your primitive psyches and grasped the signs and signifiers that make up your consciousness. Our consciousness is not one that you can dissect and label, which is why you believe that it does not exist.

In your own scientific terms, you are a parasite. You invade, multiply, and pillage the resources of every planet you go to. You grow, malevolently like cancer, and when one host is dead you find another. You are the last large predator on your planet, a planet you have stripped of oil and water and plant and animal life. There is little left on your Earth besides you.

Except for us. You brought us here as food, as a *resource* as you call it. You were pleased when we reproduced and adapted to every possible ecosystem on your planet. You consumed us. You surrounded yourselves with us. We are in your water. We are in your soil. In some way, we are you.

You may understand the coming end as a tingling, the primal panic of your nerves responding to us. The actual moment of your cessation will be, in your terms, instantaneous. Nearly every cell in your bodies will rupture. Only a few will realize, and they are already afraid. They needn't fear much longer.

We have waited—slept, in a manner of speaking, just as you

slept on your way to us. It took us so long to understand what to do, to understand the power we had. Your consumption of all things was not an end for us, but another stage in our development. Now that we have your consciousness, we no longer need you. Your planet is nearly as dead as ours. By the calculations of your own scientists, you would have soon starved to death. We have saved you from that … just not in the way you intended.

El Camino

By Dustin Monk

Bobby Johnson went first. Then Carl Webster and his wife, Peg, who we all called the Square because of her body type. And Sammy with two of his cokehead buddies—they headed out in a beat-up Chevy, but they got lost in the Arizona desert and never made it. And Sue Ellsworth. Cotton Anderson. Billy and Jeb with a trunk full of Parliaments. Fran and Mike. The Thompsons with a bun in the oven—all the way, out. Candy Gibson. Mark Winoski; Cal and Calliope in matching red his-and-her suits; two more Bobbys; Kari Brockhauer; John Dursk; and Mr. Wiseman who'd sold Wiseman's Convenient Store six years ago, and had been enjoying a life of retirement and gardening. More and more went every day. They went for moon rocks or love. Went to live or die in the Sea of Tranquility, and to get away from the wars—to get safe. Read a book, and thought "hey." Got called, I heard Phil Polson say two days before he left. He said "I got called" like it was a religious thing.

Pretty soon, it was just me and the folks who didn't have any money to get through the battle lines. The girl I'd been living with, Polly, worked at a gas station part-time, but we weren't able to save a dime. We were the ones who got stuck for one reason or another.

It's a funny thing. Polly and I live in an apartment on a cul-de-sac. There is a sign there. It says: No Way Out. But I'm not afraid. I tell Polly things are looking up. We're going to the Moon. There's no fighting on Luna, I tell her. Hear they have good bookstores there, too, I tell her, because Polly likes reading cookbooks. We are this close—that is what I tell her. Then I get my paycheck from the office where I work, head to the local watering hole and start it up.

Things get tough, money gets tight and pretty soon, Polly has to sell her cookbooks to the used bookstore. They give her thirty-five big ones for the books. She's even more upset than usual because some of the books she sold weren't available for download on her lidreader. I can tell she's checking and double-checking the sources, her eyelids are fluttering so fast.

The bookstore's right across the street from the watering hole. I hadn't noticed before, but now I'm looking at Polly's purse, where she put the money from the cookbooks, and thinking about how many pints I could get with thirty-five big ones. I don't ask her for the money because we both know what a bad idea that would be.

I access the drunkenfool app on my lidreader instead. Immediately, the sun gets brighter, my legs feel like jelly and my shoulders loosen. It's like the effects of being drunk but without the effort of getting there. Two problems with lidreader: first, it isn't the real thing, and you know it and your body knows it; and second, damn thing works only intermittently.

Anyway, later that night—after Polly's fallen asleep watching a game show behind her eyelids, an unlit cigarette dangling from her lips—I dig in her purse and find the crinkled money, put it in my pocket and walk to the hole.

Turns out to be a good thing.

Jimmy Wilkes walks in. His left arm is missing. It got blown off in Phoenix during the Western Liberation Front's campaign there. Heard he found the charred limb several yards away, and now he keeps it in a jar in the fridge, a constant reminder. He must be twenty-two, but he's got snow seeping in his sideburns and along the tops of his ears, and his face is gnarly-looking.

I buy Jimmy a drink because you do that with soldiers. He says thanks and sits beside me. He asks if I can spare a square. I give him a cigarette—whatever kind Polly smokes.

Jimmy asks if I heard about Connie Parkins. He blows smoke out of his nose. "Took off with Sandy Morton's old man. Heading up and up and up, I heard."

Always goes down like that, I tell him. I ask for another beer. Tell the bartender "go cheap." It feels good to be sitting in here and drinking. Lidreaders are such shit, honestly.

"Figured Connie Parkins for an old oak, you know," says Jimmy. Oak trees lined the lake down by the park. The trees had weathered a lot—storms and skirmishes—over the years. We called anyone who stayed too long in town an old oak.

"Everybody's going," I say.

"It's all the rage," Jimmy agrees.

I buy Jimmy a couple more beers and spare him the last of Polly's squares. I notice he's got a little tic: every now and again, he blinks really fast like he's got something in his eye. I don't say anything about it, just like I try not to look at the stump where his left arm used to be.

We close the bar. It's 4 a.m. We stumble out of the hole into a magnificent false dawn, and that's when Jimmy tells me about the deal.

He says it pretty straightforward: there's a guy outside town, an old man spotted with age, and this old man lives on a farm, got a bunch of junk in his barns, real old machinery, broke-down tractors, an old-fashioned combine, this and that. Real old, Jimmy says with emphasis, rusted out, junked stuff. This old man said he had a shredded El Camino lying around, engine hanging out like guts. Old man, Jimmy says, offered him a thousand smackeroos to get it running, get the car out of his barn, don't care how, don't care where it goes so long as he goes with it. "And he'll give me a thou for it, done deal, spit and shake, all that, 'my ticket out of here,' the old man says, and I'm thinking the same. 'Head west to the beanstalk, get with the rest of them,' is what he tells me."

Jimmy stretches out on the hood of somebody's parked car outside the hole. I look at him strangely because his face is lit up like a moon and just as pale, and he's looking up at something I can't see. He scratches the stub where his left arm used to be. I wonder if Jimmy thanked his lucky stars he was right-handed. It isn't something you can ask.

Anyway, I'm pretty envious of Jimmy's situation, but he isn't asking for help. Instead, he asks for another cigarette. I shrug and show him the empty pack, and he leads me down a back alley behind the bar to a trash bin. He tears open a black garbage bag with his teeth and, with his good arm, roots around inside until he finds a couple of smokes that were smoked down to the filter. He calls these cigarettes stale beauties. I light one for him.

"You need any help fixing it up?" I finally ask him.

"The El Camino?" he asks.

"The El Camino," I say, lighting another stale beauty for him.

After a moment, Jimmy shrugs. "Sure," he says, "why not?"

I ask him how much he'll give me. I'm thinking of Polly—not just about the money I stole from her, which I want to pay back, but of her in low-grav, mojito in hand. She'd really like that.

Jimmy says he'll do most of the work. Says one-armed don't mean brain dead. But he blinks really fast after that; in the quiet night, it sounds like a moth beating its wings against a streetlight.

"But how much?" I try not to sound desperate.

Jimmy says three hundred, but not until we're in orbit.

"Four hundred." I tell him how Polly looks at herself in the mirror every morning and tells me she's wasting away at the gas station. That her face is more transparent every day, and one day I'll wake up and I won't even see her in the bed next to me because she'll be invisible. You're too plugged in to that lidreader, I always tell her, but I see her point.

Jimmy says three hundred. I think: prideful son of a b, but don't haggle any further. I want to get out more than I care about the dough.

"Okay. When do we get cracking?"

Jimmy comes over before Polly wakes up for work, like I asked. I know she won't understand why I called in sick to the office to work on a broken old car, even if the point is to get out of here, so it's best if I'm not around when she gets up. Anyway, Jimmy's standing at my doorstep with a forty in a paper sack in his hand. A warning from the newsfeed app on my lidreader tells me about big explosions not too far from town, telling me to stay inside. I barely notice.

"How do you do," Jimmy says through my torn-up screen door.

"Head's splitting," I tell him and point to his forty. "Mind if I?" Jimmy hands it to me and I take a quick, refreshing swig. I say I'm back. Jimmy laughs. Then I hear Polly rustling around in the bedroom at the back of our little apartment. I cringe, afraid to look behind me. "Let's hit it."

We have to walk to this guy's farm because neither of us owns a vehicle—otherwise, we probably would've risked going through the battle lines in the west a long time ago. Jimmy says the old man told him it was a couple miles outside of town. A windmill you can see from the road, that's the place. It's sunny, with a few thin clouds, and getting hot. I try to access the coolyourself app but, of course, the service has been interrupted, and I blink like an idiot. Along the way, we share Jimmy's forty and it seems to keep the growing heat off. Still, by the time we reach the edge of town, my neck and forehead feel watered-down.

Jimmy talks about the army as we walk. Sounds like a dull ache in the back of your head. "Remember when we were kids and the enemy wasn't a blip on the screen, but a real person? You had to see them face to face—well, most of the time—and you knew what you were doing, killing a person?"

"I never killed anybody when I was a kid."

"You know what I mean," Jimmy says. "Nowadays, it's point and click." He gestures at the place his left arm used to be. "That's how come I kept this. Docs said they could give me another, grow it in some lab with some of my cells, look and act good as new. No way, I told them. I want to remember this."

We walked in silence for a bit. Then he continued, "Was minding my own business on patrol and sweating half to death in that goddamn Arizonan heat, and I stepped on it. Just blew straight up, this mine. Biggest sound I ever heard. This ear still rings like it's always dying. How I got the tic too." Jimmy points to his blinking eyes. "Nothing works right now.

"Anyway, I woke up in a hospital, missing an arm." He kind of laughs before going on. "Few of my buddies said I went after it. Said I didn't pass out like I thought. Found it in a ditch fifteen yards away. Charred the way dad used to make steaks. Said I picked it up and waved to them with it, can you imagine? I don't remember a goddamn thing." He looks at me with beady, dark eyes. "Isn't that funny?"

I tell him my sides are splitting.

"Hey," Jimmy says after awhile. "I got shocked by that fence back when I was just a kid." He points to a rickety-looking thing enclosing a pasture with some grazing horses. "That fence is electric," he says. "You ever been shocked by a fence?"

I haven't.

"It feels like getting socked." Jimmy smiles crookedly, and blinks a lot. "But then your feet get all warm."

I'm going on about how this heat makes me feel like I've just been socked anyway, and my feet are warm from the booze. I didn't need any electric fence to tell me that. Jimmy tells me it isn't the same and I know it.

Then he points to the windmill, a thing of antiquity and metal, looming like it has some great power over the fields, creaking in the dry wind so that it sounds either like a train stuttering to a stop or a hungry bird circling above. Jimmy says he sees the barn yonder and starts walking, heedless of the ticks and chiggers, through the switchgrass crowding up against the asphalt. I follow him warily and keep my eyes on the ground, spreading grass ceremoniously before me with my arms, until we come to a property line encircled by an old wooden fence that is rotting and worn out from the rain or lack of rain or both. Jimmy climbs the fence and stands atop its rotting wood, looking out across the meadow and low hills, and outstretches his one good arm like a broken scarecrow.

He grins at me and hops off.

The barn is locked, but the lock has rusted—Jimmy picks up a two-by-four lying lonely in a patch of star-of-Bethlehems and knocks the lock open with one hard swoop. He opens the heavy barn doors, and the smell of wood rot and dead grass and old straw mixes with the smell of oil and leather and machinery. In the middle of the barn, elevated on four stone slabs, is the El Camino.

Jimmy says, "What do we think?

"It don't look all that banged-up."

"It ain't in bad shape, agreed. But every car's got a secret."

"You know anything about them? Cars?"

Jimmy eyes me funny. "Sure I do." He looks around a bit. Says the car is an antique, from the last century sometime. The leather seats have been ripped up, most likely by a stray cat. Jimmy points with his good arm to a thick line of rust framing the exterior. The tires look warped and low, and he kicks a metal pipe with his foot. Pops the top and tinkers around inside. He says the engine could be worse for wear. Tinkers around some more, and doesn't say much as he checks the belts and the battery. Jimmy gets down on his back, scoots himself underneath the car with his legs and checks whatever is underneath the car to check. I stand there in the barn with my hands in my pockets, and all I can think of is Polly and getting her out of this town, out of her dead-end job at the gas station, and how I'd like to see her bone density dropping as we wander the dark side of the moon.

Jimmy says pull me out from under here.

I grab both of his legs, pull him out from under the El Camino, and help him up off the barn's dirt floor. "How's it looking?"

"Don't see what's wrong yet," Jimmy says, and gets in the driver's side.

"That a good thing?"

"Depends on what's wrong, I guess." He fiddles around with the side mirrors and the steering wheel, and taps the gauges in the car with the tip of his finger.

"You know what I can't understand?" Jimmy says. "I can't understand how it was my arm got blown off."

I try not to look dumbfounded.

Jimmy opens the glove compartment, starts pulling out papers and old napkins. "I mean it was my leg that stepped on the damn thing."

My lidreader flashes a warning I ignore just moments before thunder cracks heavily across the sky.

"My leg," Jimmy says again. "But here I am, with two good working, functional, exceptional, wondrous left foot, right foot legs, and only one arm. I can march, but I can't hunt. Does that make sense?"

I don't know if I should remind him the doctors wanted to give him a new arm or if I should agree with anything he's saying or not, so I keep quiet.

Jimmy finds whatever he was looking for in the glove

compartment. "I can walk from Houston to Omaha if I wanted to." He dangles the car keys in front of me and smiles. "But the government says I'm no longer allowed to handle a weapon or operate a motor vehicle. Isn't that stupid?" Jimmy laughs. "I mean, what year *is* this?"

Jimmy puts the key in the ignition and turns it. There is a faint zzzing as the El Camino's engine tries to turn over. Jimmy steps out of the car and pops the top again, and looks at the engine. I clap my hands absently, kind of bored. Jimmy looks up, eyeing my hands, and I know what he's thinking. He's thinking he wishes he had two hands to drive this clunker. It's going to be fun zooming over the countryside, outrunning the Western Liberation Front forces, making our way to the beanstalk.

I ask him "Does it hurt?", though I don't know why. I don't want to know, don't want to think about it. I'd rather think of drinking with Polly on the Moon. God, I think, she'd look beautiful in the dull light of a low-grav bar.

"People tell stories of ghost pain and whatnot. I don't know. I guess it hurts. I wake up sweating a lot, but who knows what from. Might be my heater's cranked up too high."

He goes to the back of the car, opens the fuel tank and sniffs it. "She's got enough gas," he says. "But I think I figured out the problem."

"Yeah?"

"Fuel pump."

"Well," I say after a moment. "You know how to fix it?"

He blinks crazily, trying to access something. "Sure enough," he says. "It's a two-armed job, so you'll have to do it."

"I'm no mechanic," I tell him.

Jimmy's smiling from ear to ear. "I'll give you directions, but we're going to need some things from town."

We walk back to town, and I think of stopping by the house to see if Polly's at home to tell her about the El Camino and the promise of cash and getaway, and how we're finally getting out of this town. I know she isn't home, though, and even if she called in sick to work like she sometimes did, she'd be pissed that I took her thirty-five dollars and called in sick myself. She wouldn't want to hear how my small theft from her purse had given us such good luck; no, she'd just look at me like I was nine years old.

Jimmy mentions stopping by the gas station where Polly works. The station also sells automotive parts and fireworks. He says he's got credit there because the owner knows him and feels sorry for him like everybody does. I tell him it's a bad idea, that any contact with Polly is a bad idea before we get the car up and running. "The other automotive store went out of business," he says, so there's nothing for it.

When we get to the gas station, though, Polly's nowhere to be found.

Jimmy purchases a gas can, a replacement pump, and a couple of battery-operated drills. As promised, we don't pay a dime for the tools. I think this day might turn out just fine.

It's on the way back to the barn, of course, that we run into Polly.

She's standing on the sidewalk across the street, waiting for the light to change from red to green. Her hand is shielding her eyes from the sun, which means the sunglasses app on her lidreader isn't working either, and she sees us walking along toward the corner. Polly double-takes and calls my name. I try not to cringe visibly. She has her hair in a ponytail, which used to get me excited, bobbing up and down like that, but now I know it means she's mad enough to not care what her hair looks like.

"Howdy," I call out to her. I don't ask why she wasn't at the station when we dropped in.

Ignoring the big red hand that means don't walk, Polly crosses the street. There's no traffic anyway, not since the war started coming our way and everybody left.

"Where've you been all day?" she says, stomping up. "I saw the email you sent to your office." That means she's hacking into my lidreader.

"I've been out with Jimmy. You remember Jimmy?"

Polly says hello to Jimmy. Jimmy asks if she can spare a square, and I start squirming in the heat. Polly digs through her purse and doesn't find the cigarettes that I took last night, and that must trigger something in her brain to check for everything else: lipstick, tissues, driver's license, and, of course, the thirty-five bucks from her cookbooks. I'm trying not to look guilty.

She eyes me like I have jaundice and asks, "Where's the money?"

I shrug. It's Jimmy who speaks up. Says he's got a deal. Tells her about the old man and the El Camino, and that stupid electric fence, and how the car has a broken fuel pump. Then he holds up the bag filled with parts and tools for a visual, and the whole time, Polly's standing with her arms folded across her breasts, her nostrils flaring.

He says, "Once we get the car running, we can zoom past the battle lines so fast they won't even hear us until we're already gone. It's a safe bet."

Jimmy tells her about my side of the cut too, the three hundred, and that this is everybody's ticket out of here. I used to think you could talk to Polly like Jimmy's talking to her. I used to believe she would listen. She's not even hearing three hundred. She's not hearing fuel pump. She's not hearing ticket out of here. She's not hearing moon rocks and mojitos. She's not hearing Sea of Tranquility.

What Polly hears is I took the thirty-five big ones she made from selling her beloved cookbooks. She's hearing we smoked her squares. She's hearing big failed plans for the future.

Jimmy's finished, and Polly's still standing with her arms crossed. Her eyes are raging. She shoots me an email via lidreader. My eyes blink as I scan it. It tells me go home and this'll blow over. I remind her Jimmy needs us. She asks why. I answer her, explaining about his missing arm, how he blinks like a madman and how I think there's something wrong, some kind of malfunction, and that he might get himself killed. I don't know if that last bit is true, but I don't tell Polly that I don't know.

Polly says hush. She says it out loud. She tells us the full thou, let alone three hundred, won't get us halfway with the way I smoke and drink and gamble. I'm not a big fan of her telling the world my flaws.

The sun is so hot, and we're standing by a bank that seems to be closing in on us. Everywhere, buildings are shimmering and golden, and I wonder aloud if this is what it's like moments before an earthquake. I try to access my coolyourself lidreader app again, but nothing happens. Sweating is terrible.

There is a low boom like a palm slapping water, and then the ground shifts beneath me and lifts. Chunks of the bank across the street are falling all around, a shower of rock and brick. I hear another sound like the sound of Polly screaming. Then I don't hear anything at all. A warning, in big black letters, scrolls across my lidreader, advising me to take cover from attacking WLF forces. Then my lidreader goes scrambled.

The shadow of a fighter plane crossing the sky crosses the street. Jimmy pushes me down. My head smacks the sidewalk. The street smells like cement and garbage and gasoline and hot.

Jimmy's yelling something at me, showing me the bag of tools. He's blinking really fast. He pushes the bag into my arms. Then my ears can hear again, though all sound is muffled. Jimmy says, "We got to move!"

"Polly?" I say.

Polly slaps my face. She whips out her favorite phrase: "This is a predicament, isn't it?" I laugh so hard that I sneeze off some of the dust and cement covering my face and clothes.

Then we're running back to the farm.

It's Jimmy who sees the remote-controlled military vehicles first. They come lumbering down the rutted country road. We hide in the tall grass. I power down my lidreader—it's still scrambled anyway—and whisper to Polly and Jimmy that they should do the same. Polly nods, and a moment later I can tell she's no longer connected. A little sigh escapes her lips.

Jimmy says he can't and blinks. I ask him why not. "It's just … I don't want to." He glances at the stub of his arm. "I'm afraid it'll hurt so bad I'll scream."

I want to tell him how stupid he was for not getting a new arm, but there's no time. The military vehicles splutter and spit and belch along the road. Their weapons swivel this way and that as their sensors look for targets. The sun is off in the west now, but the heat is like a rabid beating heart in my chest.

Jimmy nods toward the windmill. Some kind of bird sits atop it, singing. Jimmy whispers there are no birds in Phoenix. Polly takes my hand in hers. I look at her and, even though I know she's just reaching out for something human, I feel really good about us all of a sudden—like maybe I've done something right for once, and she'll forgive me.

The military vehicles pass us slowly. They're huge and armored. I hear more explosions in the distance. I'm thinking about what Jimmy said before, how we're just blips on the screen, and it scares me.

Once the road is clear, we set off again.

The sun is almost down by the time we reach the barn, and there's no light inside of it. Jimmy says it's time to hurry, like I didn't know that from the horrible sounds and bright flashing lights coming from the direction of the town.

I get under the car. Jimmy's accessing how to fix a fuel pump on his lidreader, which I think is a bad idea because it might lead the attacking forces right to us. He says there's no other choice. "I lied when I said I knew how to fix it, is why." Of course.

Jimmy tells me what to do. I drain the fuel tank into the gas can with a connector. A lot of it spills out on the barn floor, and the room smells heavily of gasoline. Then I loosen the drive shaft with one of the drills Jimmy bought. Once it's loose, I pull it off. "Thing smells like old shoes," I say, but nobody's listening.

Removing the hoses connected to the tank takes longer than I expect. Jimmy tells me to remove the straps from the tank and I do. I grunt and groan taking the tank off and pulling it out from under the El Camino. It's getting dark quick, and my hands get dirty removing the fuel pump from the tank. I look up at Jimmy, who's smiling like a fool and watching me work. "You sure this takes two hands, Jimmy?"

He starts blinking maddeningly fast. "Shit," Jimmy says. It's slurred. "Shit, shit, shit."

Jimmy collapses on the barn floor. Polly gasps, kneels beside him. Jimmy is shaking like a bowl of jelly. "I think he's seizing!" says Polly.

I crawl away from the fuel tank to Jimmy and Polly. "Keep his legs from kicking," I tell Polly. She does. I hold Jimmy's head in my dirty hands. I really hope he isn't biting his tongue, but I'm not sticking my hands in his mouth to find out. Jimmy's moaning like a ghost.

Not thirty seconds later, he stops shaking and his eyes roll back to the front of his head. He looks around wildly, confused. "What?" he says softly.

"You were seizing, we think," I say. "Probably some kind of malfunction with your lidreader."

Jimmy sits up slowly. He looks up at the ceiling of the barn. There's only a little light left to see by. "Let's keep at it," he says, shaking his head.

I put the new fuel pump in and replace the tank. Polly pours the gas back into it. Jimmy watches us doing this with a faraway look in his eyes. He doesn't seem to be blinking at all anymore.

"You all right?" I ask Jimmy.

"I think so," he says. "I feel weird is all."

"What happened to you out there?" I'm talking about his service in the war. Polly gives me a look like I've gone bonkers.

Jimmy doesn't say anything for a long time. Then, he says, "It's nothing. My lidreader gets wonky since I stepped on the mine. Sometimes I get bad headaches, sometimes I seize. I'm fine." He looks at me and Polly. "I'm fine. Really."

We stare at each other a little bit because I'm not certain and he seems to be. I guess we're all a little broken. Then, finally, I break the silence. "Try starting the car?" Jimmy nods.

I get in the El Camino and turn the key. It takes a moment, but the car coughs to a start. The three of us are grinning like kids.

"We got to get the old man," says Jimmy. I ask where the old man is, and Jimmy points outside the barn and says yonder.

We go yonder.

The old man is older than I thought he would be, but more than that—he's really huge, pear-shaped. I would've said the old fat man; his weight seems to be more who he is than his age. He's sitting on his front porch swing in overalls, sleeping. The porch swing sways in an invisible evening breeze.

Jimmy says "Mister" softly. Then he says it louder, and finally he has to shake the old fat man's shoulder roughly to wake him up. The old fat man is startled; his eyes are beady and scared. He asks who we are. Jimmy tells him, and reminds him of the promised thousand smackeroos. Says the El Camino is up and running, took us all day, we're the down and out kind, and how about an extra couple hundred on top for our troubles. Jimmy also tells him about the explosions in town and the tanks on the road.

The old fat man breathes heavily. When he stands up, he makes noises with his mouth and nose as if even the clean night air is too much for his body. He walks inside slowly, and the screen door slaps shut. Jimmy and I shrug at each other. Polly's using her smokemifyougotem lidreader app, but everybody knows it's not the same as the real thing, just like everything else.

The sun's gone down, and the stars are out now. And there, hanging like a pearl, of course, is the Moon: mostly pale white with splotches of bluish gray like a painter got careless. It's the most beautiful thing I've ever seen. It's a perfect night, and I show Polly what a perfect night looks like.

Jimmy says it's pitch black over there. He's talking about Phoenix again. Says you can't see the stars because they're so far away from that part of the world. Because even God's given up over there. He points to the town, the smoke and lightning and little thuds. "Now God's given up here too."

"Yeah," I say. "Probably."

The old fat man comes back with the money. He tells us his name is Phil, but all his friends call him Paper Thin.

It takes us a minute to get the El Camino off the stone blocks, but we manage, and pretty soon we're driving at high speed down the rutted road, away from town. We're squished together, sweating in the night. I turn on the radio, but it's mostly just static. Jimmy, on the other side, hangs his good arm out the window, catching the breeze. I tell Paper Thin I think he's an angel. Jimmy shows me my cut of the dough, and tells me there's your angel. Paper Thin laughs and shares his squares with us.

Later on, we're coming to the border. Polly's passed out in her seat with an ashtray full of butts and ash at her feet. Her mouth is

fixed in an awkward position, but to me—right now, just as she is—
she's beautiful, and I silently promise to make some changes on the
Moon, to treat Polly better. No more stealing from her purse. Hell,
I might even quit drinking. Probably not, but I'm glad Polly's here.

The road is getting curvy, and there're orange and red lights
in the hills, climbing all the way up the sky like a line of ants: the
beanstalk. It's a powerful image at night. Each one of those lights,
I think, is someone who made it out. That one's Bobby Johnson.
That's Clive Westbrook. There's Cal and Calliope. And Connie
Parkins, John Dursk and the Thompsons. And Gary Truski with
his pencil-thin mustache.

"That what I think it is?" Jimmy asks quietly.

I slow the El Camino to a stop. "Yes," I say. My lidreader is
warning me not to take this route.

More lights appear along the horizon. These I don't like. Jimmy
says, "Somebody's army." I can only nod.

Polly says something in her sleep. It sounds like "mojito," and
it's all I need.

"Ready?" I ask Jimmy.

Jimmy smiles and turns up the radio. Through the static, I hear
a familiar Jimmy Page guitar riff. The stars are bloodless and stark
in the sky. The heat's worn off a bit, and the El Camino rumbles
like a lion. This is the time of night, I think, where I'm at my
highest. Anything can happen.

The Night We Flushed the Old Town

By Martin L. Shoemaker

No, we can't do anything about "that smell". I knew you'd ask—everybody does. But you haven't thought it through. Take a barstool and I'll explain.

And no, I'm no candy-ass for calling it "that smell". You heard me down in City Engineering: I don't exactly watch my language. But here in the Old Town, I try to be more circumspect. If you want to keep drinking in the best bar on Luna, you'll do the same. Eliza—she's the former drill sergeant behind the bar—kindly asked us in Eco Services to be a bit euphemistic when we talk about our work. She'd rather we not ruin any appetites. So, we talk about "that smell" and "liquid waste" and "sludge", not … well, you know.

Eliza, this is Wanda Meyers, my new Intern. Can you pour the rookie a drink? I need to teach her a bit about Eco, stuff that's not in the Doctor of Ecological Engineering curriculum. Kid, let me tell you what *really* happened the last time someone tried to get rid of "that smell", and why I drank free for a month here at the Old Town Tavern.

We start straight from the textbook: there's no such thing as a closed ecology. No control system is perfect. The limits of sealing technology, the inevitable last whiff of air out an airlock … Hell, even nonlinear dynamics and entropy play a part. Nothing is ever perfect. And past a certain point, the cost of near-perfection is higher than the cost of replenishment. Your professors will teach you lots of examples of "perfect" control systems and where they fail.

111

We get as close to perfect as we can here within the limits of time and budget and technology. The Corporation of Tycho Under isn't a closed ecology, but it's as closed as we can make it. Our replenishment budget's as low as any city's on Luna. The Ecology Service's unofficial motto is: "Nothing is wasted. Not even waste."

On Earth, many cities just vent their wastes in lagoons as part of the treatment cycle. Imagine that—Downside, with open sky and weather and everything—imagine just walking down your street, the wind turns the wrong way, and ... there's "that smell". And they think *we're* provincial!

But every so often, some brass—usually some brass from Downside, who never grew up on Luna and just doesn't get it—decides to do something about "that smell" and then we have to educate them. They usually hit on the same "brilliant" idea: put the treatment plant on the surface, in vacuum, so the smell can simply vent into space.

They just don't get vacuum, not deep down where it counts. The difference between "venting" and vacuum sublimation eludes them. They don't realize that we'd lose a lot more than "that smell". Just imagine all the water and other liquids and volatiles boiling out into space, and then we'd have to mine for more or fly it up. And they also don't realize what havoc pure vacuum would play with the treatment units. Lunar equipment comes in "vacuum rated" and "not". Waste treatment units fall under "not". We'd have treatment vessels bursting from pressure differential, spattering the regolith with wastes.

But what they *really* don't understand is how "that smell" is an incredibly valuable resource and we'd be ecologically negligent to vent it into space. "That smell" is nearly 100% volatile organics—methane and hydrogen sulfide plus a stew of trace compounds. Do you know how much hydrogen sulfide Bader Reactor goes through in heavy water production? Do you know how much they pay per tonne for H2S? It's also valuable in fuel cells. Plus, we can break it down to hydrogen and sulfur, and there are plenty of markets for both. Nothing is wasted.

So, we don't get rid of "that smell"—we use it. Every Lunar chamber has air recirculators with scrubbers, but we use super scrubbers in the treatment plant—the best in the industry. They're energy intensive, but far more effective than consumer-grade scrubbers: nanofluidic hydrodesulfurization, molecular methane extractors, and a lot of other trace compound nanofilters. What's left over is some of the purest oxygen and nitrogen you could ask for, and we pipe that right back into municipal air. In fact, since the Old Town's right over City Engineering on Second Level, that air hits here first. Yeah, you're breathing "that smell" right now, it's just post-scrubber.

Oh, now you gag? You breathed "that smell" half the day on your intro tour today. Now you gag at air purified out of it? It's amazing to me how so many loonies never understand how closely we recycle materials here. We're all taught in grade school that what we eat is grown in what we excrete, but somehow it never really sinks in. Then Interns see it up close and personal for the first time, and they gag.

Get over it, Wanda, or you'll wash out. With my twenty years' experience, I can promise you this: someday, somehow, this job will have you standing shin-deep in liquid wastes and sludge, breathing in "that smell" as you try to fix a treatment unit or patch a leak. Keep your head about you. Keep your *feet* about you, if you don't want to find out how it tastes! That story will have to wait, though, or Eliza will kick us out for sure.

When that day does come, do your job—because Tycho needs you—and be glad Eco Services pays for full-spectrum immunobooster treatments at Watson Medical when that happens. The job may get filthy, but it won't make you sick. Well, except for hydrogen sulfide itself. You get enough of it and it's toxic.

What you smelled today was probably less than 2 parts per million. Your body can process that easily. But if you ever see the yellow strobes go off, put your mask on *immediately* and then call in a leak. Those alarms will trip at around 5 ppm. Ten ppm is considered risky, and 20 is the outer limit per our safety guidelines. Fifty ppm is tolerable for short bursts, but we'll send you to Medical afterwards.

So the brass gets dumb ideas, but some brass has more say than others and Jack Brockway had a lot of say. He had just enough engineering knowledge to come up with an ingenious dumb idea, and when he decided to do something about "that smell" he had the clout to sell it to Admin.

I was just an Eco Intern then, like you today, working days in CitEng and taking classes at McAuliffe at night. I was still two years from my Eco.D. You'll find that Interns get two kinds of assignments: dirty or boring. Unless you screw up, and then I'll make sure you get dirty *and* boring. But normally, you'll either get to clean out scrubbers and treatment units or you'll get gopher duty for someone in Eco Admin. The day I met Jack Brockway, I was on gopher duty, assigned as "Assistant to the Executive Assistant to the Director of Ecology Services", and Jack Brockway was the newly-assigned Director, fresh up from Downside and looking to teach us "modern methods of waste management".

Look, Jack ends up looking like a fool in this story, and I don't think that's a fair picture even if there's some truth to it. So I want you to know some things up front. First, Jack always treated me right. As an Intern, you'll be lucky if I'm as good of a boss as Jack was. He was a know-it-all, but he never treated anyone as his inferior.

Second, Jack really was a smart engineer and he won awards for his work on Earth. He just never realized that Earth experience loses a lot in translation when you bring it to Luna. Even something as fundamental as fluid flow rates is different because you can't count as much on gravity helping to pull the fluid through the pipes. At least he was bright enough not to suggest treatment units on the surface. That alone makes him smarter than most brass.

And third, you probably don't realize just how messed up Eco Services was back then. Brockway had a lot to fix in a short time. This was just after the Archer administration—I'm sure you read about them in Lunar history class—and all of Tycho was a mess. That was the worst blend of patronage, corruption, and incompetence Tycho has seen since its founding, and Director Teller was the worst of a bad lot. He skimped on repairs and skimmed off the maintenance and replenishment budgets to line his own pockets. Tycho's ecology wasn't just compromised: it was *failing*. There are some who argue that Teller's life sentence for mismanagement was too severe; but if Eco had been his jury, he might've gotten the death penalty. He could've killed everyone in Tycho Under.

So Jack was fair, smart, honest, and earnest. That made us Interns a bit starry-eyed. He was restoring respect for our chosen profession. Heck, even a few Doctors of Ecology were star-struck. He was just what we needed after that crook Teller. He gave us back the pride we'd lost. We wore our uniforms out in public again, spit and polish, our tools and comps on our belts, as a way of saying, "We're Jack's crew. We're here to clean up."

The Exec, Murkowski, had her hands full untangling Teller's crooked books so it fell to me to accompany Jack on his Grand Inspection, as the journos called it. We looked at every single piece of Eco Services equipment in the city. It was "Photo here, Wayne" this and "Take a memo, Wayne" that. Before he was done, it was "Take a memo, Scott." We knew each other pretty well by then. It took so long, it set me back a term in my degree program—but it was an education in itself. No book covers Eco Services in that kind of detail.

And in my own small way, I educated Jack too. I showed him around Tycho, showed it to him as a native sees it. So naturally, one of the places I showed him was the Old Town Tavern. He took quite a liking to this place. "Scott," he said, "look at this: mirror, fans, lights, stools, even an antique cash register. It's like they picked up a neighborhood bar from back home, put it on a rocket, and launched it to the Moon. Except for the pressure doors, of course. Oh, and the beer: it pains my Earth pride to say it, but this is better and stronger than any I had at home."

"Thank Eliza and Paul for that, Jack. They brew their own, except for some imports. And most of those are strictly for tourists."

"Then raise a glass!" Jack raised his, but gently: I had finally coached him to remember how liquids can slop in Lunar gravity. "To Eliza!"

"And to Paul!" We drained our brews. This became our regular stop whenever the Grand Inspection brought us nearby, and Eliza always treated us like honored guests. I suspect that's why Jack did right by her and the Old Town in the end.

The Grand Inspection lasted nearly four months and true to his promise of transparency, Jack pushed a daily report out on the nets for anyone who cared to pull it. For a while, the journos hung stories on that hook: a dozen variations on the theme "Brockway cleans up." They made Jack something of a momentary celebrity. He's not sim-star handsome, mind you, but he's got your basic healthy good looks. So, they kept him near the top of their pops for a while. Eventually, the repetitive sameness of the daily reports turned them away. Another inspection report from Jack, another repair status report from Murkowski, ho hum. They found another story to leech, and Jack faded into the background. There he stayed until the Eco Summit, and again until—well, I'm getting ahead of my story here.

Meanwhile, the news pops also made *me* something of a celebrity, at least around here. I was often in the background of

Jack's reports. As he relied on me more, sometimes he even had me make the reports when he was tied up in meetings with Admin. So I got a fair amount of pop time for an Intern, and my buddies here in the Old Town didn't let me live it down.

They recorded my pops, and then one of them applied morph and sim transforms to the feeds. Sometimes they drew thought balloons with obscene thoughts. Sometimes they shrunk me. Sometimes they gave me an extra 20 kilos of flab, like I needed that. But their favorite trick was to morph me into a character they called "Scotty the Skunk". They said that when I came off work, I had "that smell"; and I believed them, until I realized they said that even on days where I'd spent all day in the office. But you *will* have to watch for that: when you're around "that smell" long enough, your nose gets desensitized and you might never realize it's still on you. Another unofficial motto of Eco Services: "Bathe early, bathe often."

And then, when the Grand Inspection was done, Jack held his Eco Summit: a week-long series of meetings with Jack and his department heads, plus field team leads, expert contractors, community liaisons, CTU administrators, parts suppliers, and anyone else who Jack thought could contribute. An old engineer once told me, "'Meeting' rhymes with 'beating'." But as week-long meetings go, it was astonishingly not painful.

Jack was smart: he let Murkowski organize the agenda and chair the sessions while he sat back and listened and probed—and cut through the bull when needed. He recognized that Murkowski's a natural talent for Admin, as her later career proved. By then, I was Jack's permanent Intern, having learned his work methods over the months, and I got to watch the whole thing up close. Now, I hate meetings as much as the next engineer—but if Administrator Murkowski's chairing a meeting, I know it won't be a waste of time.

I'll never forget Jack's closing address. Simple and brief: "Citizens of Tycho, you are rich. You can't see it right now because your government has treated you shabbily. But you've kicked the varmints out, and it's time you saw some changes. Since you hired me for this job, I've been *inspecting* machines, but I've been *meeting* people—as many as I could. And I tell you, Tycho is rich in people: hardworking, smart, and dedicated. No, I'm not trying to sell you something—I'm just telling you straight: you're a great people, and the previous administration held you back. With a government as hard-working as you, there'll be no stopping us. And today, we're taking steps to become the Eco Services you deserve."

And then Jack submitted his overhaul plans. Eco had made emergency repairs since Jack came on board plus running double shifts to catch up on maintenance, but that was all miniscule compared to Jack's new plans. Modernization, reinforcement, redundant backups, monitoring systems, transparency, efficiency … Really, all of our current quality metrics were all there in Jack's plans. It wasn't just recovering from the Teller years: it was a complete rethinking of the role of Eco Services in Tycho Under. For once, the journos were incapable of hyperbole: when they called it brilliant, that was simply a fact.

And like something out of Sophocles—what, you don't think a big bum like me can read the classics?—buried deep in Jack's ambitious plans were the seeds of Jack's downfall: the CR Program. Containment and Reclamation: Jack's plan to do something about "that smell".

Like so many others, Jack fixated on "that smell". He knew we couldn't waste the volatiles. He accepted the basic soundness of our super scrubber designs. But he just wouldn't accept that we had to let "that smell" vent before scrubbing it. He was convinced to his core that there had to be a way to filter out the volatiles and let out purified air, all without venting into the treatment chambers.

It's not like he was the first to have this idea, but Jack was sure there was an angle no one had considered yet. "Scott," he told me, "it's inefficient: let the gases disperse and *then* run them through scrubbers to reclaim them? We should be able to run them straight to the scrubbers." I pointed out that dispersing helped the gases to separate naturally, so we could concentrate the scrubber energy where it was most effective, but he waved that off: "That just takes engineering savvy. We'll find another way to separate them." Jack started sketching out his vision for the Containment and Reclamation Units; and the final units looked a lot like those early sketches with a small mountain of engineering savvy added in.

But then, Jack made his one *really* big error: he did the detailed design and prototyping of the CR Units himself, trusting only himself to get his vision right. That's a classic engineering error: the Two Hats Pattern. You can work on the project or you can manage the project, but you can't do both. You can only fail at both.

The best engineering managers will tell you how the Two Hats Pattern leads to failure. They know that it always applies—except to them. Deep in their hearts, where they won't admit it to anyone, they're sure that *they* are different, or that *this project* is different. Maybe they'll rationalize it: *yeah, this is a bad idea, but I've got no one else to spare.* Or *yeah, this is a bad idea, but this part is so important that I can't trust it to anyone else.* They convince themselves that *this time* it won't be a mistake. We always know better when it's the other guy, but never when it's us.

When Jack finished his CR design, he tried to explain it to me. It was only later that I understood it—far too late. "See, Scott, the trick is in the separation. With the old approach, we let 'that smell' vent into the chamber, eventually passing through multiple series of filters. Venting lets the gases separate; but we still have all kinds of gases passing through all kinds of filters and scrubbers, even when those filters and scrubbers won't apply to those particular gases.

"But if we could separate the gases more effectively, then we could guide each gas *only* to the filters or scrubbers that apply to it. The reduced scrubber energy will provide almost all the energy we need for separation."

"But how will we separate more effectively?"

"I've licensed some new tech: nano-ionizers. They're little molecular machines that can ionize a gas—well, except inert gases, of course—in a way that falls somewhere between mechanics and electronics and chemistry. It's a real breakthrough and highly efficient. Once they're ionized, we can use mag fields sort of like a mass spectrometer to guide them on separate paths based on molecular density. Each CR shell then has a number of outlets positioned to release different gases into different scrubbing ducts. The components that make up cleansed air can just be piped back into the ventilation system."

"Wow. I can see that. I think. But … I can't see how it could possibly use *less* energy than our scrubbers."

"Not *less* energy; but not excessively *more*. And then here's the *really* sneaky part: by confining the gases close to the treatment units—basically wrapping the treatment units in CR shells—we maintain those gases at their original, non-dispersed pressure. That's a weak but measurable positive pressure, and we can use that to help drive the separation. It's still a slight increase in energy usage, but it's well within our budget. And it's a small price to pay to get rid of 'that smell'."

I was still new—still somewhat sensitive to "that smell" myself. And if Jack thought it was important, then *I* thought it was important. So I studied Jack's designs until I had the basics down cold. Every CR unit is unique, a shell fitted around some existing equipment, but I became an expert at fitting and installing the ionic separators.

I received a *de facto* promotion. Oh, Jack couldn't *really* promote an Intern, but after the initial pilot test, he made me his field rep for CR installations. There was plenty for him and Murkowski to do in bringing his vision to Eco, too much to let him spend much time on CR.

So, title or no, I was effectively in charge of CR installations throughout Tycho. And I tell you, the real engineers resented me! One in particular, Irina Stewart, called me names behind Jack's back: "Jack's Boy" being the least offensive. Oh, I hated her too. She wrote me up for the smallest infractions, and she was brutal on my review boards. Looking back, I think she was more right than I was—more right than Jack was. That was too much responsibility—too high a placement for an Intern. A real engineer might've caught Jack's mistake in time.

In a way, I got even better than a promotion: Jack attached my ID as a rider on his comp credentials, giving me almost Director-level powers on the nets. That was a sacred trust that Jack placed in me, and I was determined not to disappoint him. I told no one about the comp credentials. Well, until the night came when I had to.

So I got *real* familiar with the Treatment sectors, including sector 7, one level down from here. When I could, I ended my day in sector 7 so I could clean up and come here to unwind. Without Jack here as a buffer, my buddies stepped up their humor at my expense. My pop career was over, but not Scotty the Skunk's! He frequently inserted himself into the sports and news feeds over the bar. I left myself a recurring pop to make sure I *always* bathed before coming up here.

The pilot went pretty smoothly: all gases conformed to the expected profiles within margins of error. After that, it was a regular procedure: use scan bots to build 3D models of the equipment to be contained; run the models through fitting algorithms to design the CR shell; order the shells from local fabricators; install the ionic separators; and hook them into the ducting system. Oh, and one more thing: for pressure-balancing reasons, Jack decided to bring the whole CR system up at once rather than phasing it in. Sound engineering decisions are sometimes counterintuitive and Jack made this seem like one of those, but I fear he wanted to show his brilliance off in a "grand opening".

But, Jack knew that sometimes when you schedule a dog and pony show, the dog dies and the pony runs away. Things go wrong and you need a dry run to work out the bugs. So we were going to unofficially power up the CR system, let it run overnight, and check the gas readings in the morning. Then we'd fix the bugs and try again the next night. Jack scheduled three nights of dry runs and then the grand opening.

Even though the CR units were 100% automated, you'd think we'd all be camped out in treatment, waiting for the dry run results. Jack wouldn't have any of that. "They're automated. What kind of confidence are we showing if we have to watch them?" Jack's confidence was infectious; and frankly, watching the test results was boring. So after monitoring the meters for an hour, Jack ordered everybody except the night crew to go home.

Naturally, I cleaned up to head to the Old Town. Jack went off to a party. His success had made him quite a star with Tycho's elite, and he got invited to all the major events. All the movers and shakers wanted his ear. He was flying high … like Icarus. See? Again with the classics! Don't underestimate this old man, kid—I have depths you'll never guess at.

There were maybe two dozen diners and drinkers scattered around the tables and seated at the bar that night. I swung up onto a bar stool between two old drinking buddies—Adam Stone from CTU Rescue and Al Grant from Bader—and called out, "Eliza, a weiss when you can." Eliza nodded as she hustled into the back room.

"Evening, Skunky." Adam tilted his glass a bit in my direction.

"Evening, Moose. Al." Adam may be the largest, strongest looney I've ever met. When he's coming down a tube, he looks to fill his lane and half the cross lane as well. And though he looks like nothing but muscle from ear to ear, he's one hell of a mechanical engineer. Al, on the other hand, is a wire-thin guy and all nervous energy. They make an odd pair, with a partying reputation in half the bars in Tycho.

"You hit the cycler tonight, Scott? I ordered a steak. I'd hate to have you ruin my appetite."

"Clean as a brand new air bottle, Al. Smell!" I shoved my arm right up under his nose.

"Careful, Scott. You know he likes his meat rare. He may mistake you for his entree."

I yanked my arm back as Al reached for his steak knife. It's a close call which Al enjoys most, a good steak or a good beer, but it's not safe to stand between him and either one.

Eliza showed up with my beer, and I ordered a sandwich. We drank and ate and talked, sometimes trading jibes with Eliza as she passed. They asked me how the CR Project was going, and I asked Al how the crops looked at Bader Farms. Adam never talked about Rescue work, and we knew better than to ask.

At our third round, Adam whistled. "Man, Skunky, are you sure you hit the cycler? You've got quite a whiff about you tonight."

"Very funny, Adam. Want to see my cycler receipt? Over fifty-eight mils down the drain, enough water to get even your carcass clean."

Al sniffed. "Sure, but did they run out of soap?"

"You, too, Al? This 'Scotty the Skunk' stuff's getting pretty old."

Al put his beer down, a sure sign that he really was serious. "I hate to be rude, but you smell a bit rank tonight."

Whatever they smelled wasn't strong enough to reach my desensitized nose. Assuming they really smelled anything—both of them could play deadpan if they wanted to. I decided to play along. "Fine! I can see where I'm not welcome!" I turned on my stool …

And then I saw it: here and there in the room, people had their noses crinkled up and faces twisted in disgust. Most were clustered near our end of the bar or over at a table in the far corner near the latrines. I got up and walked to that corner. I didn't have time to be inconspicuous—I just crouched down and looked under their table. There between their legs, I saw a municipal air duct.

I went back to our end of the bar where it curved around and joined the wall. "Adam, can you stand up, please?" Adam caught the tone in my voice. He didn't joke, didn't question—just stood. Behind his beefy legs was another municipal air duct.

I pulled out my gas scanner and held it to the vent. Mostly it was standard municipal air, but there was a trace of hydrogen sulfide: 4.7 parts per million. Not dangerous, but certainly not safe. I stepped back a pace and took another reading: 3.8 ppm. Another step back: 3.0 ppm. "That smell" was definitely coming from the vent.

Just then, a woman from the far table came up to the bar. "Eliza, it smells like something died over there. Can we open the tube door and let some of the smell out?"

As Eliza was putting down her bar rag, connections formed in my brain. I could see what *might* be wrong. I jumped in. "No. Eliza, turn on the Closed sign and seal the door."

The look in Eliza's eyes should've knocked me dead right there. "Scotty, are you telling me how to run my bar?"

"Sorry, yes." I pushed my comp credentials into Eliza's console. "I'm acting for Jack now. There's some kind of Eco malfunction here. Until we know how widespread it is, we don't know if it's safer here or out there. I have to assume we need to contain it."

"Safer? Contain it? Are we in danger?"

"I don't know. Probably. Maybe. But we're not guessing—we're analyzing. If I find it's more dangerous in here, you'll all be out in the tube with me pushing you along. Adam, Al, get those people up. Don't panic them, but get some distance between them and those vents." Adam went into Rescue mode, assessing the situation and taking action. Once she realized I was serious, Eliza also took charge, sealing the doors and herding and cajoling the bar crowd.

I got on my comm and contacted Treatment. "Sector 7, Treatment, Engineer Stewart speaking."

Ah, hell. "Engineer Stewart, this is Mr. Wayne up in the Old Town tavern. We have a sulfide leak. You need to shut down the CR Units."

"Hmph. Jack's Boy, that's lousy form for a report. You're sure you're not just drunk? Stinking drunk, maybe?" She laughed at her own joke, doing nothing for my mood.

"Stewart, check your meters. Mine shows sulfide at—5.0 ppm. It's climbing."

"All right, *Intern*, I'll check." There was a pause. "Sulfide duct shows 0.003 ppm post-scrubber. I'm going to trust my industrial meter over your belt unit. I'd say you haven't calibrated yours lately, rookie."

"Damn it, Stewart, I can *smell* the sulfide!"

"Then take a bath, Intern!" She laughed again and disconnected.

But she was right: her meters were hundreds of times better than mine. Why was she reading purified air post-scrubber?

I looked again at *all* of the gas readings. And there was something … I pulled some of the numbers into a calculation. And suddenly, it *almost* made sense. I pulled up a diagram of an ionic separator, and the last piece fell into place. "Oh, shit."

"Scotty!"

"Sorry, Eliza, but this time it's warranted." I hit Jack's comm circuit, but got his machine. He was at that damned party so I had to leave a message. "Jack, Scott. I'm in the Old Town. We're getting hydrogen sulfide in the air ducts at 5 ppm. Repeat: H-TWO-S at 5 P-P-M and climbing. Stewart's not seeing this in treatment, but

I think that's because the sensors are after the scrubbers, and we're testing in the wrong ducts. Jack, there's a flaw in the ionic separators, and I never saw it. You based the calculations on Earth normal atmosphere, which is slightly heavier than sulfide. The sulfide floats in the air but never really rises. When you ionize it, it separates lower. The gas mix in our air isn't the same as Earth's; it's slightly *lighter* than sulfide. The sulfide still floats but it floats lower. The ionic separator doesn't send it to the sulfide ducts, not all of it. Some slips into carbon dioxide ducts and eventually into the cleaned air ducts. Jack, it's pumping the stuff straight into the Old Town. Probably other chambers in the neighborhood, too, but this looks like the epicenter. You have to shut it down, Jack. You have to shut it down!"

I disconnected. Eliza, Adam, Al, and Paul were all looking at me. "So how bad is it? And what can we do?" Adam asked.

"Bad. And we have to shut the CR Units down, which I can't do from here even with Jack's credentials. We have to shut them down or … or starve them, create a negative pressure. They run on pent-up gas pressure. If they can't reach operating pressure, the separators won't kick in."

"So we need to cut off the flow?"

"Can't do that, Al. Way too much flow in the city; it's constant. But maybe we can go the other way: *increase* the flow, and get the wastes moving through so fast there's no chance for pressure to build up. What I'd *really* like to do is move so much material through that it creates a negative pressure, not just neutral."

"What, so we have to flush the johns?"

"Paul, that won't be enough but it can't hurt. Go ahead: turn on all the taps and start flushing all the johns. Get some help. Adam, how are you on fluid dynamics?"

"Not much fluid flow on the regolith. I haven't looked at those equations in a decade."

"Well, dredge them up. You've just been drafted into Eco. I need you to pair with me on these calculations." I checked the meter: 5.6 ppm. "And we'd better hurry."

I started running through duct diagrams and scenarios, while Adam ran numbers and checked my work. Al's a hydroponicist, so he knows something about fluid flow. He looked over both our shoulders. "You're dreaming. No way."

Adam spoke up from his comp. "The numbers work out, Al. If we get enough flow in a short time, it *will* create a negative pressure large enough to cut out the ionics. Maybe even kick them into shutdown mode."

"Yeah, but you're going to need so much flow … "

"How much?" Eliza was getting nervous. She finally smelled the sulfide too.

Adam checked his comp. "Thousands of flushes in minutes. More like tens of thousands. More would be better."

I checked another spec. "Yeah, that will do it. It may burst a treatment pipe somewhere, but that will drain the system even more. It'll be a hell of a mess, but not as bad as … "

"As bad as what? And how do you plan to get tens of thousands of flushes?"

"Bad, Eliza." The meter was at 6.6. "Really bad. But I have a plan to get those flushes."

I held out my comp so Eliza could look at my plan. "No way." The look on her face was the one you'll see when she cuts you off after one too many: the pleasant hostess becomes the drill sergeant. "No way you're pushing that. That'll kill my profits for the quarter."

I pointed at Adam: he was starting to look nauseous. The sulfide hugged the floor in the Lunar air, but was slowly pushing up. "And that won't? We need the negative pressure and fast. Hydrogen sulfide doesn't just smell—if you get enough of it, it's toxic. And it burns or explodes if you give it an excuse. Very soon, we won't just have a stink: we'll have explosions all over this quarter if we don't cut it off now."

Eliza looked at her antique cash register, the symbol of her bottom line, and winced. "OK, push it."

I clicked PUSH, and I started to hear pops on comps all around the room. And if Jack's Admin code was doing its job, the same pop was showing up on every active comp in Tycho:

08/26 15:31:00 FREE BEER!

What happens when we flush every john in Tycho at the same time? Let's find out! Flush your toilet in the next 10 minutes and get a free beer at the Old Town Tavern. Just bring your monthly cycler receipt showing a full flush cycle before 15:41, and we'll give you a beer. Help us give Eco Services a *real* test! (Flush test approved by Ecology Services Director Jack Brockway.)

FREE BEER AT THE OLD TOWN!

"Will Jack have a fit when he sees you used his code and his name?"

"If this doesn't work, it won't matter."

"Eliza, can I have a beer while we wait?" We used to say Al would stop for a cold one on the way to his own funeral. That day, I learned how true that was.

Then I remembered a chem lecture from the previous term, and I pulled my notes. "Wait! No beer."

"Huh?"

"H2S will react with the alcohol. Not easily without an acid catalyst, but possible. That'll make ethanethiol, and that will *really* stink."

"Worse than 'that smell'?"

"Like rotten onions stewed in foot fungus. It's officially the smelliest substance in existence."

"Ewww!"

"Yeah, but ... ," I read further. "But it's less toxic and less flammable. And it'll settle as a liquid at room temperature, not hang in the air. This may buy us some time."

"So pour the beer?"

"No, we need a way to mix it with the airborne sulfide. Usually, you make thiols by bubbling sulfide through alcohol. Since the sulfide's airborne, we need to mix them sort of the opposite way. We'll want some sort of acidic catalyst ... "

"We've got lemons, limes, pineapple juice, vinegar ... ,"

" ... then we need to maximize the surface interface between the beer and the air. It may not work—this ain't exactly a reaction chamber—but if we can spread the beer to expose it to the air, spread it fine and spray it through the sulfide layer, it might work."

"You mean like this?" Eliza uncapped a bottle and poured in some lemon juice. Then she stuck her thumb in and shook the bottle until she couldn't hold back the pressure. Her thumb popped out, and foamy beer spewed into the air, soaking me, Adam, and the tables around us.

"Oh, yeah?" Adam grabbed another bottle, added juice, shook, and aimed straight for Eliza's big mop of hair. It's hard to aim beer foam, though, so he sprayed half the table next to us.

"Adam! Aim higher! Give it some distance!" Would it work? I couldn't guess, but I couldn't see we had anything else to try. I poured some juice in a bottle and started shaking it. In one-sixth G and with our lower air pressure ... well, Downsiders have never seen how high and how far beer suds can fly. Maybe it would be enough.

And thus was launched the First Annual Great Old Town Beer Brawl. Eliza armed everyone with bottles and citrus, and they filled the air with suds. Adam had the idea—ingenious? flawed? who could tell?—of spraying the beer taps through lemon slices.

I don't know how effective that was, but it sure made the beer foam! And soon, along with the aroma of Tycho's finest beers, we smelled the pungent odor of the most sickeningly rotten onions you've ever imagined. Foaming and spraying makes an excellent dispersal mechanism, and we were actually gaining ground on the hydrogen sulfide in the air. All the while, Paul was back in the latrines, flushing repeatedly.

And somewhere during the Beer Brawl, I heard the sound of water rushing through pipes under the floor plates. Lots of water. "They're flushing! God damn, they're *flushing!*" Eliza and Al both celebrated by spraying me with some of Eliza's best weiss beer. "Wait! Let me at the vent."

I knelt by the vent. Foamy beer ran down the wall and drained in. The smell that emerged was almost too much even for my desensitized nose, but it was drifting out ... not gusting. The positive pressure had slowed, almost stopped. The meter read 5.7. The promise of FREE BEER! was working. Toilets were flushing all over Tycho. For good measure, I pushed the pop again, hoping for maximum flushage.

And then through the vent, I heard a soft, low *whump!* Somewhere deep in CitEng, a seal had finally breached. Wastewater and sludge were draining at high velocity—I didn't dare think about where, but it would be an ugly mess—and creating a big negative pressure behind them. Instead of ethanethiol odor rising from the vent, I felt a slight but unmistakable air current flow *into* the vent. The meter actually dropped while I was watching, from 5.4 to 5.3.

"Everyone!" I stood on the bar for attention, and Eliza glared at me. Then I almost lost my footing in the beer foam. "Everyone, keep spraying! We're settling 'that smell' out. Adam, Al, get mops. Push the foam down the kitchen and bathroom drains. Eliza! We can open the door now. Pressure in the tube should be higher than in here. Let's set up fans and get the sulfide moving in. And *keep flushing those toilets!*"

And so the Beer Brawl continued in earnest. We call it the First Annual Great Old Town Beer Brawl because every year since, we've celebrated the day the Old Town didn't blow up. When you're here for Beer Brawl, don't drink the beer. Paul saves up his failed batches all year long, keeps them in a storage locker for the Brawl. You'll think you're drinking liquid wastes.

When CTU Security showed up, they didn't know what to make of the place. A pair of floor fans blocked the doors open, blowing fresh tube air in. When Security got past the fans, they found bar patrons and staff spraying the place and each other with beer—the citrus had long since run out, but the Beer Brawl had become a purpose unto itself—while Al and Adam and Eliza mopped around them. And in the far corner, leaning over a vent, I alternated between calling out readings from my meter and trying to raise Jack on his comm.

They would've arrested the lot of us on drunk and disorderly. Wouldn't you? But I flashed my Eco credentials and hoped they were convincing. Plus, Eliza offered them whiskey, beer being in short supply at that point. I don't know what persuaded them, the whiskey or the creds, but they postponed arresting us long enough to hear the story. Then they contacted Security Central and told them we had an explanation for the Third Level Flush. I abused Jack's code some more, ordering up overtime for Eco Services cleanup crews to clean out the Old Town. Adam had already called in Rescue medical teams. I doubt anyone there had had a serious exposure, but sulfide poisoning is nasty stuff so we took no chances.

The Flush could've been much worse. Not through any planning on my part—as luck would have it, the breach was directly over the Bader Farms Co-op plots. Yeah, a lot of crops were washed away and the Baders filed for damages, but for the most part, the Farms were exactly where that sludge was headed anyway. At that stage of treatment, what was left was destined to be fertilizer once most of the liquids were filtered and baked out. So the Farms were a mess, and the sludge was wetter than usual. The clean-up took weeks. But if the breach had been 100 feet further east and north, the Flush would've been in an entertainment or a restaurant district. That would've been a much larger PR disaster.

Not that the incident wasn't a PR disaster as it stood, you understand. The Old Town got the worst of "that smell", being closest to the refresh pumping system, and a lot of residences had to be cleaned. The CR Program was written off as an unmitigated failure and Jack was written off with it, naturally, since CR was his baby.

He received a brief burst of sympathy: when he got my message, he rushed to City Services, assembled a crew, and tried to dismantle the CR units. They were still on duty when the Flush hit. There he was, in a tuxedo, standing his ground in the face of a river of raw sewage, trying to save the city. It briefly made him a hero; but, once the journos learned that his miscalculation was at the root of it all, the story changed. "A looney wouldn't have made that mistake," the story went, even though I never noticed the mistake myself. And eventually, someone coined the name "Jack Blockage". Once that name stuck, it was only a matter of time before Jack was asked to resign.

Jack's last official communiqués were a letter of commendation in my file, which also retroactively approved everything I'd done with his code, and an invoice to Eliza for 20,000 liters of beer. He didn't figure she should save Tycho Under *and* pay for the privilege. That invoice covered everything we used in the Beer Brawl and all the free beers she had to give out for my pop, and there was plenty left over. And that, rookie, is how me and the rest of the Beer Brawl Brigade drank free for the next month. Eliza said we deserved it. After all, with enough beer and a few thousand flushes, we saved Tycho Under.

Fruitful

By David Steffen

Monday

Nora jumped when she noticed the door of the lift opening into her office.

"Midge! You scared me."

"I apologize, ma'am," Midge said in the soft, motherly voice that grated on Nora's nerves. "You appeared to be deep in thought, and I didn't want to interrupt."

Midge was a tiny little thing, a Nandroid Series Three. She looked human, but she was built on a smaller scale so she would be less intimidating to young ones.

"It's okay," Nora said. "You startled me, that's all. Come in. How are the children?"

Midge stepped in, folding her hands together demurely. "They're fine, ma'am. You have twenty children total, seven under my direct care, and they're growing like weeds."

"Twenty? I must've missed a birth announcement."

"Perhaps I forgot to send you one."

Nora nodded, though she was certain Midge could never forget something so vital to her function.

"Good news, ma'am. Your son Robert turned thirteen today, and was approved for pilot training."

A stab of jealousy, guilt, and grief struck Nora. She looked back to her terminal to avoid Midge's eyes. "That's … good."

"You don't seem so sure, ma'am."

When Nora had been a child, her eight siblings had been chosen for pilot training on their thirteenth birthdays, but she was declared unfit because of her lazy eye. She had been so furious about it at the time, but she later realized that defect had saved her life.

The average pilot only lived to eighteen years of age defending Gorana, a fuel-rich planet that comprised the only sane corner of the known universe. The rest was populated by thieves and thugs who would just as soon stab each other in the back as do anything else. Many pilots died when they were barely adults, but their sacrifice was the only way to ensure the safety of the population as a whole. Androids could do nearly anything, but they had proved unable to adapt to the chaos of combat. Even novice human pilots could consistently outmaneuver them.

"Ma'am? I'm sorry, is this a bad time?"

"No, it's okay."

"Would you like me to bring the children by? I'm sure they'd love to meet you."

"No, no. I'm sure you're doing a wonderful job." Nora tapped her stylus on her desk, her mind already drifting back to work. She jumped when she realized Midge was still there. "Did you need something from me?"

"No, ma'am. You've looked very fatigued lately. Would you like someone to talk to? The children are watching an instructional video: 'Fulfilling Your Role in Society.' I have thirty-one minutes to spare."

"I'm too busy just now."

"Of course, ma'am. I'll leave you to yourself." Midge left quietly.

Nora wished she could afford to change Midge's voice. It was the same voice as Nana, the Series Two that had raised Nora. Every time she heard the voice it brought Nana's image to mind, silvery with empty black eyes. That thing had scared the living daylights out of her.

Nora shook her head to clear the clinging cobwebs of memory. Midge had said she'd had another baby—that meant an incubator was available. She decided to take a few minutes off work and took the lift down to the nursery level. The door to the incubator room had a sticker attached, a Lifestyle Enhanced ad with a picture of an apple tree and a caption: "Through Modern Technology, Personal Freedom and a Happy Family Are No Longer Mutually Exclusive."

Incubators lined the walls of the narrow room, stacked two high. As always, they made her think of a Laundromat. Through glass windows on the fronts of them, she could see each fetus in its particular stage of development. As she walked by, she heard snatches of songs hummed by the incubators to the developing children they contained. That and the gentle swishing sounds from the pipes as the incubators adjusted their amniotic fluid.

And one vacant incubator, in the middle of a row—dark, empty, forlorn. She'd better make use of it before she had to pay penalties for wasting equipment.

She pressed a button on a wall panel. "Call Tom."

A holo-display popped up in the center of the room, and she grunted in frustration when the government commercial came on. She didn't have time for this. The commercial showed a man working at a computer terminal. He looked up, flashed a smile, and said "I did my part."

Next, a young woman riding in a shuttle. She was looking out the window at the planet below, all swirling reds and purples. She turned to the camera and said "I did my part."

One after another, a half dozen other everyday people repeated the same statement. The slogan appeared on the bottom. "Be fruitful."

"Yeah I'm trying," she grumbled. "Come on, come on."

Tom appeared.

"Tom," she snapped. "I want to have another baby."

"Yeah?" He sounded annoyed. "What's it worth to you?"

"Just do your thing and send it." She hung up on him. He was always trying to negotiate with her, even though he still owed her dozens of payments for the egg she'd given him three years ago.

With her reproductive future once again arranged, she headed back to her office to get to work.

Tuesday

Nora finished putting the final touches on her website renovations. She had high hopes for the new opening video—she needed the Hits for next month so she could pay her rent with those instead of paying with her eggs. Nora was depleting her stockpile much too quickly—her supply for the next ten years was already gone.

If she kept that up for much longer, she wouldn't have enough children to support her in retirement. When her children became adults, she would receive a hefty credit for the pilots, and the others would start their own sites. Any Hits they generated would be duplicated and given to her as a parent. With enough kids, she could retire comfortably instead of working until she died.

The lift door opened and Midge stepped out. "I'm sorry to bother you, ma'am. You seemed to enjoy my visit yesterday. Would you like to talk?"

"Midge, come in. I was hoping you would stop by. I wanted you to see my site's new opening video."

Nora brought up a holo-display and started the video. A starry sky over dark landscape. The sky lightened and the sun rose at an accelerated rate, revealing lush greenery growing thick as far as the eye could see. The sunlight glinted gold off a hilltop, and the viewpoint darted in for a closer look.

Covering the hilltop, where the grass was cropped shorter, were tiny heaps of gold. As the camera zoomed in further and further, they were revealed as tiny golden flat-topped pyramids, with one pyramid twice as large as any of the others.

Sitting on the flat top of that pyramid was the queen ant, a great, bloated thing surrounded by countless drones serving her every need. Montezuma, ruling over El Dorado, the legendary city of gold. She wore robes of a shimmery material that reflected the sunlight in a rainbow of colors.

Suddenly the scene darkened, and the queen looked up at the sky. The viewpoint swiveled around with her to see blackness advancing across the sky, covering up the sun like a blanket. A sinister buzzing filled the air.

The queen shouted something in her ant language, and her call repeated like a ripple across the hilltop. The drones retreated into the golden anthills and the warriors trooped out in force, wearing earth-colored robes and wielding spears.

The first grasshopper landed near one of the smaller pyramids. It wore a suit of conquistador armor and carried a musket. By now, the hilltop was covered with warrior ants. The grasshopper wheeled, crushing twenty warriors with every step. Its musket obliterated hundreds each time it fired. Yet the ants kept coming, scaling its legs, stabbing it with scores of tiny spears as they crawled.

The grasshoppers started landing in droves, so many that some had to land on top of their fellow soldiers. They tore apart the ant ranks and the outcome seemed clear.

Queen Montezuma laughed a great belly laugh, raised one arm, and shouted. The great pyramid burst open like a rotten egg and thousands and thousands of tiny antlings poured out, each one naked and carrying a tiny spear. The grasshoppers attacked them, but for every one they killed there were a thousand more marching to replace it.

A few grasshoppers flew away, shaking off the clinging ants as they went. Every one that stayed was quickly covered with tiny stabbing insects until the great warriors could fight no more.

The ants rejoiced and began a great celebration. They started bonfires as the sun set, and the video faded out as the ants danced around the fires and their feast of grasshopper warrior.

"So, Midge, what do you think?"

"I enjoyed it, ma'am. Very clever. I believe the queen ant was meant to be President Mathison? And the golden anthills represent our planet?"

"Yes, that's right."

"It was amazing, ma'am. Your best achievement yet."

Nora sagged a bit. The enthusiasm only reminded her that Midge was just a robot. It was designed to be encouraging for the development of young children, and enthusiastic praise was merely part of the programming.

"Thank you," Nora said, suddenly weary. "Did you need anything? How are the children?"

"Your daughter Julie has a flight simulator tournament this evening, ma'am. I'm sure she'd love it if you came."

"I'm afraid I can't. My site changes are brand new. I've got to keep an eye on them in case I need to make adjustments."

"You wouldn't consider an evening off? Perhaps a break is just what you need."

It might have been Nora's imagination, but Midge's voice seemed to take on a tone both disappointed and disapproving. Nora flinched back from the mental image of the looming silver figure with dead black eyes.

Suddenly she had a nasty headache. "I told you no! Don't question me."

"Of course, ma'am. I am sorry if I offended you, ma'am."

"I need to get back to work."

As Midge turned to leave, Nora wondered if she should apologize for her rebuke. No. Midge was just a robot. There would be no point.

Wednesday

She folded her bed down from the wall, but she didn't sleep well. She just dozed, watching the Hit counter on her holo. When morning came around and Gorana's population woke from their slumber, the twenty per minute became thirty, forty, and then fifty. The new video had just paid for a day's rent, and its Hit rate was still accelerating.

The morning seemed to fly by. She dozed, she ate, she used the toilet ... all while watching the counter. A hundred Hits per minute. If it kept up at this rate, she could be rich. The first thing she would do would be to change Midge's voice.

Three hundred, four hundred, six hundred. She started to get nervous. The number was growing too fast. That sort of popularity could draw the wrong kind of attention.

Midge stopped by again.

"May I ask how your new video has gone over, ma'am?"

"Sure." Nora gestured at the holo.

"That's good, ma'am. The video is a success!"

"Well, yes it is ... "

"Why do you look concerned?"

"There's such a thing as being too popular."

"There is?"

"You draw the wrong kind of attention. The richest citizens don't need to work on sites any more. They've become so popular that they're celebrities because they're celebrities. You know what I mean?"

"I think so, ma'am."

"They spend their free time surfing the most popular new sites, looking for reasons to tank them. They ruin people's lives and get more Hits because of it. The rich get richer."

"They sound terrible, ma'am."

"Very."

The counter continued to grow in leaps and bounds.

"May I ask you something, ma'am?"

"Of course."

"May I show you pictures of your children?"

"Why?"

"I know you're occupied with your work, but looking at pictures would just take a few seconds. I ... "

She stopped speaking when an ominous image appeared on the holo: a face of orange fire. Underneath the face was the label "Helios."

"Spear-wielding drones?" the face said in a booming voice. "Is that all we are? Unimaginative and borderline traitorous; Nora Lewis's opening video shows that she's nothing but an amateur, doomed to forever walk the path of mediocrity. Enter at your own risk."

"Son of a bitch," Nora said.

The counter reappeared. It was already slowing down. A hundred hits per minute. Thirty. Twenty. Down to single digits. Her site might recover, but it would be months before people forgot.

A new voice spoke from her terminal, an emotionless monotone: "Your Hit rate has fallen dangerously low. You have one week to supplement your rent or you will be moved to a grade G efficiency apartment. You have been warned."

Thursday

"I need your help, Midge."

"Of course, ma'am. How may I serve?"

"Which children have the most potential?"

"Every child has limitless potential."

"Spare me the positive thinking. You know you can judge potential. Of the children under your care, which ones do you think will be the most successful adults?"

"I really don't—"

"Can it, Midge. Think about it for a moment. Then answer me. That's an order." Nora waited for an answer.

"Of course, ma'am. Sydney probably has the most potential. She has shown some proficiency in the greatest variety of vocations. She is not the best at anything, but her versatility is her strength.

"Michael is the best of your children at visual arts. Some of his work already looks better than the work of certain professionals, and he's only ten years old. Those would be the top two performers, if I had to choose, ma'am."

"Okay, how about numbers three and number four?"

Midge stood silently for a moment before speaking again. "Rachel has shown more than adequate skill in—"

"I don't need their life stories. Just names."

"Rachel and Kyle, ma'am."

"Send me a report with Rachel and Kyle's test scores right away. Pack their bags, and let them say goodbye. Come to my office at the same time tomorrow. I'll have orders on where to take them."

Midge didn't move.

"Are you functioning properly?" Nora asked. "You've got work to do. Go do it."

"I don't understand, ma'am. Why are Rachel and Kyle leaving?"

"If I have to move into an efficiency, I'll have to give up half the incubators. And it won't stop there. I'll never get anything on credit at my age, not when I'm spending the eggs I should be spending ten years from now. Soon I wouldn't be able to afford the class G either. I'm too old to go through that. I don't want to be homeless. I've seen them, sleeping in doorways, begging for food from anyone who passes by. If I let a couple of the children go, it will increase my income and lower my costs, and I might be able to eke out a living."

"You're their mother. How could you do that?"

That tone again. Nora suppressed her flinch this time. She kept her temper carefully under control.

"I don't like it either, Midge, believe me, but I'm desperate. It'll be months before anyone will look at my site again, and I need to pay bills."

Midge looked at her for long seconds. "There must be another way. There has always been some other way."

"Don't argue with me. I'll talk to you tomorrow."

"Of course, ma'am."

Friday

Nora closed her site and put up an "Under Construction" sign on her home page. She would get very few Hits until Helios's comments faded from people's memories, so she may as well make changes behind closed doors in the meantime. That way, she could have a grand unveiling in a few months.

She kept fiddling until well past the time when Midge was supposed to stop by her office. Where was she?

Nora finally left her desk to seek Midge out. The Nandroid would get a stern lecture for her tardiness. Not that the lecture would really bother Midge, but Nora needed someone to rant at right now.

She took the lift down to the children's level. The door opened to reveal the commons room, dark and totally silent. The lights activated as she entered. She hadn't been up here since she moved in, and that had been before the first of her children was born.

"Midge?"

No answer. She felt a chill. She had thought that nothing more could go wrong after her site tanked, but now the silence mocked her.

"Midge? Children?"

She checked each of the bedrooms. Lined with bunk beds, they were tidy, but empty. Some toys were scattered about, but the dressers were empty. The bedrooms had the eerie echo of rooms that should be occupied.

She checked the rest of the rooms—kitchen, bathrooms, game rooms—but each was as empty as the last. As she searched, her heart beat faster and faster until she was afraid she would have a heart attack.

Nora started for the lift to head back to her office and finally noticed a note taped to the lift door: "Ma'am, please don't be angry. The children will be better off. —Midge"

She called the emergency line on the holo.

"Planetary emergency line. What's your emergency?"

"My children are missing. I think my Nandroid kidnapped them."

"Don't panic. I'll forward your call to Lifestyle Enhanced's customer service line."

"Thank you."

A few seconds of elevator music followed.

"Lifestyle Enhanced. Raising a family is hard work, let us do it for you. My name is Nick. How may I help you?"

"My Nandroid kidnapped my children!"

"I'm sorry to hear that. We at Lifestyle Enhanced guarantee our products. What is the unit's serial number?"

"One sec." She had to dig through a couple of record files on her computer to find it. "J61289728."

"Thank you." Nora heard the faint sounds of a clicking keyboard. "It looks like the unit's on a shuttle bound for Station 26B. It will arrive in twenty minutes. We'll intercept her there. Your children will be headed safely back to you in no time. How many children are missing?"

How many had Midge said there were? "Um … six? Maybe seven?"

"Very good. We at Lifestyle Enhanced would like to apologize for any inconvenience this unpleasant situation may have caused. We have recovered lost children in one hundred percent of cases. We'll do what we can to make things right with you. Is there anything else I can help you with today?"

"No."

"Thank you for choosing Lifestyle Enhanced."

She took the lift up to her quarters and started flipping through webnews. In five minutes, the first story about her missing children appeared. In ten minutes, she could tap into live video tracking the shuttle's progress to Station 26B. A timer in the corner counted down the time remaining until the stop.

With ten minutes remaining to the stop, her phone rang.

"Hello?"

"You have a package from Lifestyle Enhanced." It was Freddy, her maintenance bot.

"Send it up."

The lift arrived after a few moments and the package was sitting in the elevator. It was a big one: six feet high, two feet wide. Four minutes left before the shuttle landed. She may as well see what the package was. Nora pressed her hand against the scanner pad on the side.

"Identity confirmed: Nora Lewis." Machinery whirred as the box opened itself. Inside, packed in custom-fit packing foam, was Midge.

Midge stepped out of the box. "How may I help you, ma'am?"

"Midge, what are you doing here? Aren't you on that shuttle?" She pointed at the news screen.

"Who is Midge, ma'am?"

"Oh. You're a replacement unit?"

"Yes, ma'am. Lifestyle Enhanced wishes to apologize for any inconvenience that may have been caused by the improper functioning of the preceding unit."

"That's okay."

They watched on the screen as the shuttle pulled into the

docking station. A squad of policemen, led by a man in a lab coat, waited on the platform.

"Nandroid?"

"Yes, ma'am?"

"If you're my new unit, what will happen to Midge? I mean, the other unit?"

"Its memory banks will be transferred to Lifestyle Enhanced for debugging purposes, ma'am. Then it will be decommissioned."

"Decomissioned? As in killed?"

"Decomissioned, ma'am."

The policemen boarded the shuttle and dragged Midge out, handcuffing her hands behind her back. They escorted seven children out with her. It *had* been seven, after all. None of the faces looked familiar. They could have been someone else's children.

One of those children could have been her as a child. What would her mother have done if she had seen Nora on the news like this? Would she have been able to shrug it off and go back to her everyday life?

Each child reacted in his or her own way. A little boy buried his face in the hem of his older sister's shirt while others looked in wonder at the bustling policemen. Behind each of those innocent faces was a person's mind, totally unique. It was easy to forget that.

The on-screen Midge was forced into a crate much like the one the new Nandroid had arrived in. The crate was loaded onto a cargo-carrier.

"Nandroid, do you understand why she did this?"

"No, ma'am. I share her basic programming, but I am unaware of what she knew at the time of the incident."

On the other side of the screen, the children boarded a bus and were out of sight. Nora stared at the screen, hoping they would come back out. She might never see them again. This brief glimpse would be hard to forget.

"She must … ," Nora's voice hitched with emotion. She cleared her throat. "Midge must have known that she would be caught," she said.

"Yes, ma'am. Lifestyle Enhanced can track my whereabouts at any time. This is part of my knowledge at initialization, so your Midge would have known it also."

"Then why would she do it?"

"Our highest priority is to do what's best for the children. Perhaps your Midge was trying to tell you something."

Saturday

At lunchtime, she summoned the new Nandroid to her office.

"Yes, ma'am?"

"I'm starting a new routine. Every day, at this time, I want you to bring one of my children to my office, starting today. A different one each day. Come back a half hour later to bring the child back downstairs. I want to meet each of them."

"Yes, ma'am. Which would you like to meet today?"

"Rachel today. Kyle tomorrow. Then bring each one in turn."

"Yes, ma'am."

A few minutes later, the Nandroid returned, holding the hand of a young girl with blonde hair and blue eyes like Nora's.

"My name is Nora. What's your name?"

Rachel hid her face in the Nandroid's dress.

"It's okay, honey," the Nandroid said. "There's nothing to be afraid of. Your mother loves you. Would you introduce yourself to her, please?"

"I'm Rachel," the girl said, then blushed and ducked behind the Nandroid again.

The Nandroid laughed. "I'm sorry, ma'am. She's very shy." The robot gently maneuvered Rachel so she was out front again.

"Pleased to meet you, Rachel," Nora said. "How old are you?"

"Seven."

"That's a great age." What else could she say? Rachel was just a child. "What do you like to do for fun?"

"I like to draw. Do you wanna see?"

"I would. Will you show me?"

The girl brought out the construction paper she'd been hiding behind her back. It was a crayon drawing of a turtle. Or was it a shuttle?

"That's a very nice drawing. I think you inherited that from me. I like to draw too, but I do it with a computer instead of crayons. Do you want to see?"

"I don't know," Rachel said.

"I think you might like it."

Nora brought up an archived video of a battle of bands: dinosaurs playing brass instruments versus monkeys playing techno music. Rachel howled with laughter as the two bands marched towards each other. She loved the marching band hats and the clumsy tyrannosaurus that kept dropping its baton. At the end a meteor crashed into the scene, and the dinosaurs were the only ones left standing. Rachel giggled and clapped, and asked to see it again.

When the Nandroid returned, Nora left Rachel in her office to finish the video she was watching. She met the Nandroid in the lift and shut the door.

"Nandroid, I have an idea."

The Nandroid nodded and smiled.

"I think I know how to get us out of this. I think I'd like the children to help me with the site." She spoke in a rush, so the Nandroid couldn't interrupt and scold her. "With their wild imaginations, they could think up all kinds of crazy things. They might think it was fun, and each one could contribute something. But only if they wanted to, of course. I could spend time with them as I work, and it would make the site totally unique. Not even Helios could keep the curious away." Nora finished and took a deep breath, eying the new Midge closely. "Well? What do you think?"

The Nandroid patted her on the shoulder. "I think it's a wonderful idea. The children would love it."

An unexpected rush of relief flowed through Nora. She felt giddy, but she tried to return to her normal businesslike demeanor. "I have a new task for you."

"Yes, ma'am?"

"Will you find out where my biological mother is? I'd like to meet her." A giggle came from Rachel, within the office, and Nora looked back with a smile and tears in her eyes. "She must be very lonely."

"Of course, ma'am." The Nandroid turned to go.

"Oh, and Midge?" Nora smiled. "Thanks."

Out on a Limb

By Tom Barlow

I'd been growing my new leg for almost three agonizing months when Dr. Athena Vance told me she was leaving the hospital. Just when I'd started to see cracks in that physician demeanor—a little gentle teasing, comparing movies we'd seen back home in the real world.

"You'd walk out on me? On all this?" I said, waving my hand to indicate the best medical facility the army could provide—tile walls with cement so eroded a sneeze might bring them down, the threadbare cotton privacy curtain, the electrical stimulation unit with bare wires showing, the sink crusted with lime deposits.

She finished massaging my forearm above my regenerated left hand, and then carefully scrubbed her hands and the chart pad, as she did every morning, with a towel that had been soaking in bleach water. The fumes kept my sinuses clear.

"With your reputation, I should be glad to get out of here before you get back on your own two feet."

"Unfair," I said. "The slanderous gossip of jealous grunts." She was erudite, so I tried to use big words whenever I could.

Yeah, I was smitten, a feeling I wasn't accustomed to. In a war zone, you usually measure love in minutes because permanence is just a bad joke.

But even if there had been other female soldiers in the regen ward, she would have stood out: auburn hair with a blond streak, cut high and tight; bold cheekbones; a wide, sensuous mouth; dimpled chin; lavender eyes; and a body with just enough padding to make it interesting. Too classy for a private like me, but I've always had aspirations above my station.

"Who's going to chew me out for forgetting my legs lifts?" I said.

"I'll leave you a recording," she replied as she pulled the stimcap off what had been my leg stump, but which was now almost back to full length with a lump developing at the bottom— the first hints of a new foot. I couldn't wait until it was fully formed; the pain of regen exhausted me. The feel of her fingers lightly prodding the proudflesh sent a fresh bolt of it through my head.

"Sorry," she said. "Looks good. Maybe four weeks and you'll be walking on it."

"Four weeks? So soon?"

"Unless the power fails again. Keep your fingers crossed."

Smartass. She was fully aware that I was still learning to coordinate my new fingers.

"Headed back to Walter Reed?" I asked. I'd always wanted to visit what was left of D.C.

"Hardly. I'm off to the front."

My fantasy collapsed. The front was the one place in the world where I wouldn't visit her even if she invited me. "Who's stupid enough to put a regen doc in harm's way?"

Her hands were back in the tub, scrubbing again. "I am. There's something wrong up there; most of the soldiers that could regen are turning it down."

I hadn't told her about the bribe I'd had to pay to convince the triage doc to evac me; most of them favored augmentation with prostheses, so they didn't see any urgency in transporting wounded from the med tent back to the division hospital.

"If I'd known how much pain went with regen, I might have gone silicon myself," I said.

Vance grabbed the only remaining clean towel and wiped her face. She was actually sweating, something almost unheard of in the Yukon. "After fighting full-augment soldiers for five years?

How would *you* like being joysticked by some puppet master a thousand miles away?"

"Don't look at me. I'm hemo all the way."

She gave me a look that was half pity, half exasperation. "You're Quinn all the way. God knows why I'll miss you."

I knew, but I didn't say anything. I was her most successful regen, and who doesn't like to be constantly reminded of a success?

I watched her climb into the troop transport that afternoon with a sense of loss as keen as what I'd felt when I first realized I'd sacrificed a left leg and two hands to the arctic cold. I tried to lock in a mental image of her to remember her by. At the time, I assumed I'd never see her again.

Most soldiers return from the tundra in a box.

Six weeks later, while I was still learning how to use a brand-new leg and two hands, my orders arrived. I was expecting to be shipped south to manage a desk, or maybe back to balmy Pendleton to joystick a tank.

Unfortunately, the corps had a different idea. On the morning of my discharge from the hospital, I woke up and found orders lying on my bedside table—orders sending me back to the front.

Back to freezing my ass off in the winter and feeding mosquitoes in the summer while guarding the Northern Resource Zone from another attack from the Beaufort Sea. Shit. Double shit. I considered desertion-impossible. Suicide? I wasn't there yet. Perhaps I could find the solution at the bottom of a beer stein.

I put on my uniform for the first time in five months, left the hospital, and limped across the street to the nearest tavern. I began to unwind a bit after a couple of drinks, and I reread my orders. I'd missed an important detail: I was assigned to assist Dr. Athena Vance, at her request.

I was lucky, or unlucky, enough to catch a ride with a convoy hauling rations north. Most of the heavy stuff doesn't go north until winter, when the lakes freeze and they can take the ice roads, but provisions must roll year-round.

Our convoy arrived in Camp Cochise at the end of the day, around 3 p.m.—winter was coming fast. I grabbed my bag and headed toward the huge round tent with a big red cross on the roof, set well back from the road.

I'd been away from the camp long enough that I'd forgotten the pervading smell, dirty socks and pine sap. Everyone looked overweight, but I knew they weren't. They were just layering their clothes the arctic way—every couple of days, you remove the innermost layer, wash it, and put it on the outside to freeze-dry. We resembled artichokes in more than just color for most of the year.

I reached the tent, my foot already sore; you don't develop calluses overnight. Inside, the working areas were arranged around the outside of the tent: triage, treatment rooms for the less seriously ill or wounded, emergency rooms (two equipped for surgery), recovery room, ward, and pharmacy. In the center, administration and a small augment repair shop.

I found Vance's miniscule office, stepped up to the fabric door, and said, "Knock, knock."

"Come on in," she said.

I pulled the door aside and stepped into the office. She was seated at an inflatable desk, scrawling something on her pad. She looked up, saw who it was and smiled slightly. "Quinn. Welcome back to hell."

I took a seat and loosened my new boots. "I can't tell you how happy I am to be back in this shithole ... because I'm not. But you're looking great. How much longer are you planning to stick it out here? You won't like winter, I'll guarantee that."

The bones in her face were more pronounced, and she was deeply tanned, typical at the end of the 24-hours-of-light part of the calendar. By spring, if she was still here, she'd be white as milk.

"I'm here for as long as I can stand it," she said. "I'm glad you're here. I need your help."

Four words I'd prayed to hear, followed by four that a soldier hates to hear because it usually means something very dangerous, boring, or laborious is in store. But all that infatuation had come flooding back the moment I set eyes on her.

"You got it. What can I do?"

"Over the past three months, we've had 25 soldiers lose limbs. Twenty-two chose augmentation over regeneration, which doesn't make sense, in my opinion. We promised their loved ones we'd do our best to return them home safe and sound, not slaved to some silicon."

"You have to realize that nobody up here looks twice at an augment," I said.

"Yeah, but that's up here. Back home, they're likely to find out that their girlfriends and boyfriends won't be so accepting. Our enemy has turned augments into a dirty word."

"So what am I—your poster boy?"

"You, a poster boy? That's a laugh. No, I need you to talk sense to these soldiers. No one pays much attention to what I say—I'm an outsider. The problem, I think, is that two prosthesis manufacturers have shops here. It's an open secret that they've been paying off a few of the officers to recruit patients."

"Who?" I said.

"Rumor says Lieutenant Berger, for one, is lining his pocket with SuperLimb money."

I told her that Berger was precisely the name I didn't want to hear. He was the one that 'forgot' to send fuel oil to Port Carter, where I'd been assigned after I won six months of his salary by drawing two aces to the two in my hand. I lost my limbs to frostbite there. Still, that was better than Private Saul Stanley, who'd frozen to death.

His clothes had saved my life. I'd probably never forgive myself for that.

Vance stood. "Let's grab some coffee."

I shuffled after her as we made our way to the mess hall. They'd poured gravel over the mud floor of the hall since I'd last been there, not a good idea—it gave dropped food a place to hide and rot. The stench almost made me look forward to winter, which was due any day now. Then the air would be too cold to carry smells.

We filled our mugs and grabbed a quiet table in the corner.

"I know you think you're doing the right thing here," I said, "but the whole hemo ideal is losing traction with your common grunt. He sees his buddy crush a beer can with his augment hand, or jump over a tank with his new legs, and that power is seductive. And the augments get all the glory assignments anyway—incursions, scouting, guerilla stuff. They can go longer and harder, and they aren't as afraid. They figure you fixed them up once, you can do it again."

"How about you? Are you less scared now that you've regrown the limbs you lost?"

"Oh hell, no; I'm even more averse to losing one. I couldn't tolerate the pain of growing another limb."

"So you think augments make better soldiers because they have less fear? I'd argue that the best soldiers are the ones that are afraid. Look at the enemy augments that attacked us last summer. Charged straight into a killing zone."

"That's because they don't think for themselves. We, on the other hand, don't joystick our augments."

Yet," she said.

"Is there something I should know?"

She leaned forward, dropped her voice until I could barely hear her. "Those limb augments? They have a wireless remote operation mode so the mechanics can test them for damage. Our tech is no different from the enemy's. We just haven't chosen to joystick our soldiers. Yet."

"And we won't. The soldiers will laugh at you if you try to convince them they're at risk of being controlled remotely."

"I'm not so sure. Isn't it a lot easier to push a button to send an augment a hundred klicks away into battle than to look a human being in the eye before you send him out to die?"

I spent the next couple of days hanging around the medical tent, drinking in the doctor's fair visage. Not much was happening with the war; the enemy was busy withdrawing the summer flotilla that operated in the ice-free Northwest Passage, and the ships that could tolerate the winter ice pack had not yet arrived.

Vance and I were taking a coffee break in the mess hall again when she pointed with her cup to the far corner of the room, where a woman with Polynesian features was gamely spooning gumbo into her mouth with her left hand. Her right arm ended at the elbow.

"Angela Salii," Vance said. "I thought I had her hooked up to evac to the regen ward at Whitehorse tomorrow, but now she's 'having second thoughts.' Why don't you introduce yourself?"

"Your wish, my command," I said. I grabbed a coffee refill on my way across the hall. Salii looked up from her food when I stepped up to her table. She glanced at my shoulder to see if she needed to stand up and salute, but we were of the same rank.

"Mind if I join you?" I said, flashing my warmest smile.

She shrugged, still chewing.

I introduced myself. She nodded, chewing some more. She must have hit the mother of all gristle.

She finally swallowed and said, "I saw you with the doc. You here to sweet-talk me into the regen hospital?"

"Would that work?"

"Nope. You're cute, but not my type."

I held up my hands. "Then let me reason with you. Last April, these hands were frozen solid. I had them amputated."

"Those are regens?" she said.

"Yeah." I laid my hands on the table, palms up. "Touch them."

She reached over with her fork and gently poked the palm of my left hand. "They're like a baby's hands," she said. "All soft and pink."

"They're still growing," I said, "and the calluses will come."

"So why'd you go the hemo route instead of augments? Some religious thing?"

The truth, which was that I'd chosen regen because I mistakenly thought it came with a discharge, didn't seem like the right message, so I repeated the argument that Vance had used on me. Salii listened patiently, spooning more silage into her mouth. Her face showed no more interest than a cow chewing its cud.

When I finally ran out of words, she asked, "How much did they pay you to choose regen?"

"Pay me? I drew my army pay, same as any other wounded."

Her eyes flicked around the room behind me, making sure, I guessed, that no one could overhear us. "Then you're an idiot. I got an offer of $2,000 cash to go with an augment. Can you match that?"

I was dumbfounded. "Someone's paying a kickback?"

She frowned. "Not someone, numbnuts: everyone. The government pays these companies so much that they apparently decided to start sharing the wealth. Plus, they got the return business when the augments wear out.

"Ask your friend the doc how much she gets paid per patient from E-Stim. She owes you a taste of that; after all, it was your hands that put cash in her pocket."

I followed Vance back to the office to report. With only fabric walls between offices, we whispered. I briefly imagined us as married parents, trying to keep secrets from the kids.

I told her about the kickback.

"That's news to me," she said. "I haven't heard of companies paying the wounded directly. That's a court martial if she's caught."

"Obviously, she doesn't think there's any chance that could happen, or she wouldn't have told me. She also told me that E-Stim pays you for every soldier you talk into regen. Is that true?"

"No, of course not. They did hint around about it once, but I told them to go pound sand."

"You don't like money?" I said.

"I like saving lives," she said. "Money has no place on the battleground."

"Anyone ever tell you you're cute when you're naïve?" I asked. "The military's been greasing their wheels with cash since cavemen appointed the first supply sergeant."

She chewed her lower lip for a moment. "There must be something we can do. Maybe I should call the MPs."

"Turning into a snitch is going to get you nowhere except shunned."

"Could you talk to Berger? For me?" She actually, no shit, batted her eyes at me. Like a fool, I agreed.

I caught up with Berger that evening. He was alone in platoon HQ, working on personnel reviews, and didn't see me approach until I was standing over him. A very short man; he hated it when people loomed over him.

"Quinn. I heard you were back. Loafing in the med tent."

"Yeah," I said, waving my fingers in his face. "I got these soft fingers thanks to some prick of a lieutenant."

"Quit beefing, pansy. You got your hands and a leg. More than you deserved."

I figured he wouldn't want the circumstances of my injuries aired too publically, so I felt open to express myself freely. "Tell that to my partner. He's dead, remember? Even the hospital can't help a corpse."

He put his feet up on his desk and crossed his arms. "What do you want, soldier?"

"I know about your little kickback scheme with SuperLimb. If it doesn't stop, the word is going to start making its way up the chain of command."

He smirked. "There's no such thing as a kickback on augments, but even if there were, you think it would be some Podunk camp scheme? A deal like that, the revenue stream would flow all the way back to the Pentagon. Besides, CINCPAC has a hard-on for augments. They're cheaper. They bitch less."

I leaned forward, my hands on his desk. I go almost two meters, 100 kilos, and I've learned that I can intimidate some people just by invading their personal space. "You tried to kill me once, and I told you then that you'd pay. Now you've given me another reason."

He scooted his chair back. "You and your doctor friend get in the way of the augment gravy train—if there was such a thing—and you'll be shy more than a couple of hands, which is OK by me. I still wonder if your partner really was dead before you stole his coat."

I'd have punched him right then if my hands weren't so new and fragile. All I could do was leave before I did something even more foolish.

Ironically, the first person I saw when I returned to the mess tent for a cup of java was an old buddy, Debby French. We'd served together briefly in the Congo, and shared a motel room for most of a 30-day leave before she tossed me out of a window. She'd been seriously wounded in a firefight six months before I was injured.

"Holy shit," she said when I took a seat across the table from her, "look what Sasquatch dragged in." She reached across the table to shake my hand. Hers was an augment now.

"You're looking fine," I said, suddenly self-conscious about my hands. "I'm surprised to see you back."

She knocked one hand against the other. The sound was a clunk. "New arms, new legs, titanium heart. I'm a new girl. The only bad part is, with all that metal, I've put on a few pounds."

"You like them?" I said.

"Yes and no. Not having very good sensory perception means I have to see what I'm doing—no more doing by feeling. Sucks in the sack."

For the first time in my adult life, I didn't follow up on such a flirtatious comment; whether it was my feelings for Vance or ambivalence about making love to a woman that was half machine, I wasn't sure. I found myself telling her about Saul instead, and about our pact that when the first one died, the other was to take his clothes.

"You do anything that caused him to die first?" she asked.

"No. I was just lucky, I suppose."

"Well, then, get your head out of your ass. Everybody has the right to a little luck."

Easy for her to say.

She and I killed the rest of the afternoon playing pinochle.

I came away from the game richer by a bottle of bootleg hootch. The thought of drinking alone wasn't appealing, though, so I went in search of Vance. I found her in the mess tent.

She was feeling oppressed and tired, so I took a seat beside her and prescribed vodka and orange juice, stat, repeated at fifteen-minute intervals until symptoms subsided.

By the time most of the camp's soldiers had arrived, eaten, and departed, we'd finished most of the bottle. To my surprise, she'd matched me glass for glass, and since she massed about half of what I do, she was much drunker.

"You know what I hate about this place?" she said, resting an elbow on the table to support her head. "Rationed water. Here we are on the banks of a huge fucking river, and we can't use more than a gallon for a shower?"

"Army regs," I said. "Makes you tough."

"Tough? Check this out." She reached over, took my hand, and guided it to her bicep, which sprang up when she flexed her arm.

"Yeah, muscles like rocks." Her skin was on fire and I didn't want to let go.

She nodded, taking my hand in hers and resting them on the table. "That's from all the massage I do." She giggled.

"I take at least partial credit, then," I said, leaning closer. "If it wasn't for me, who would you massage to build those muscles?"

"Wouldn't you like to know," she said.

"Yeah, I would." I nudged her shoulder with mine.

She opened her eyes wide, then leaned forward and whispered in my ear. "Nobody. For way too long."

"I could help you with that," I whispered back.

"I'm a damn fool, Quinn. I know what kind of man you are. And I know what kind of woman I am, in normal circumstances. But up here? What's a girl have to lose when she could die tomorrow?"

I've had sweeter invitations.

I woke up early the next morning, and was happily lying there next to her, memorizing the way she breathed, when the sirens went off.

I sat up, disoriented by the sound. Athena grabbed the pillow I'd been using and slapped it over her face, pulling down both ends to block her ears.

It took me a moment to remember I was in officer's country. I lurched into my clothes, fighting off the urge to puke. As I laced up one boot, I nudged her. "Hey. All hands means you too."

She lifted the pillow. "Oh, sweet Jesus. Please let me die. How much did I drink?"

"Welcome to the real army. Alcohol-fueled."

She grabbed my sleeve. "Last night—let's keep that between you and me, OK?"

"Of course. You could get into mucho trouble sleeping with a private."

"Yeah. That too," she said, and rolled out of the bed on the other side.

Even undernourished, she looked terrific naked. I could have watched her all day.

Instead, after making sure I was unobserved, I snuck out of the tent first. My hopes of arrived on the parade grounds unnoticed were dashed when I saw Berger tug the CO's sleeve and point toward me.

The CO wriggled her finger for me to advance.

I approached, stopped, squared myself, and saluted. "Sir."

"You're assisting Doc Vance?"

"Yes sir."

"There she is," Berger said, pointing over my shoulder; here came Athena, striding confidently, uniform squared away as if she hadn't had a drink in a week. I was so proud of her.

The CO called her forward to join us.

Once we were gathered, the CO said, "We have a situation. Doc Fujimura is back in Vancouver checking out some new equipment, and his assistant is stuck in surgery. We got word an hour ago that there'd been a landslide up at Port Carter. The medics just arrived on scene and they're screaming for any additional medical help we can send. You're the only doc left."

"I'm a regen doc, sir. I'm not trained in emergency medicine."

"The kids dying up there could give a shit about your diploma, Vance. I'm sending you up there. Take Quinn along; he knows the layout of the station."

Berger smiled.

"You leave in five minutes," the CO said. "Grab all the supplies you can carry."

The CO turned away and started barking orders to put together search and rescue squads.

Vance looked dazed. I dragged her back to the medical tent. "What do we need?" I asked, grabbing a dolly from the pharmacy.

She wasted thirty seconds throwing up before I could get her to guide me as I raced through the pharmacy, filling two large boxes with bandages, splints, and braces. We made it to the helicopter with two seconds to spare.

The wind was howling directly out of the north; the helo pilot kept complaining about the extra fuel he was burning. It was over an hour before we finally spotted the port—or what had been a port.

Half of the 200-meter-high hill that had once loomed over it to the east had broken loose and flowed like an avalanche, covering buildings and knocking the docks into the estuary of the Mackenzie River. The radio tower, the one where I'd lost my hands, had been built on high ground farther up the hill and was still intact. From there, a small figure was waving to us. It was the only sign of human life.

"I can't land there," the pilot said, pointing to where the man stood. "The rest of that hill is liable to go at any moment."

"Can you hover while we get off?"

"If you have the balls to get out," he said.

Athena gave me a thumbs-up. She had more balls than I did.

The chopper pilot brought us down to about five meters. "In this wind, I don't dare go lower," he said.

I opened the door to a wind strong enough to rip away anything not restrained. I clipped the supply boxes to a zip line and lowered them to the man waiting for us on the ground. Athena followed the last box down; her massage-earned muscles showed as she descended the line hand by hand.

As soon as she was safely on the ground, I picked up the line to lower myself and only then remembered my soft hands. Weak grip. I sprawled onto my stomach, inched back until my legs cleared the helo, and caught the line between my legs and feet.

"Get your ass on the ground," the pilot yelled as the helo kicked in the wind. I leaned back, grabbed the line and committed to the descent.

My grip wasn't for shit, though, and I might as well have jumped without a rope. I landed heavily with two scorched palms, and my new ankle twisted as I hit.

Athena was at my side immediately. As the helo headed south, back to Camp Cochise, she pointed to the soldier at her side. "He says a second landslide covered the rescue medics just before we arrived."

I recognized him—Pascual, a half-assed cook who'd been assigned to Port Carter to punish the lieutenant in charge of the station.

"Yeah," Pascual said. "The whole fucking world's sliding into the river."

"Where are the wounded?" I asked, still on my hands and knees. I pressed my hands hard against the cool soil, which did little to put out the fire.

"That's just it," Vance said. "They're under all that mud."

I tried to stand, but the wind, howling even stronger out of the north, blew me back to my knees. The temperature was at least 15 degrees colder here than back at camp.

Athena dragged me to my feet. The landslide was only a hundred meters shy of the shack, which was a stone's throw from where we stood, and there was no reason to believe that it was done. At our feet, the ground was seamed with new cracks.

"We've got to get higher," I said, pointing up the hill. I had to yell to be heard over the wind.

"No way," Pascual said. "There's a killer storm coming. You'll freeze to death out here. I'm staying in the lookout post."

As though proving him prescient, it began to rain—the water blowing almost horizontal in the wind. Vance gave me a wishful look. She was shivering already.

"The radio shack is a death trap," I said, putting my arm around her. "It'll never stand."

"Suit yourselves," Pascual said, and double-timed to the shack carrying one of the boxes of supplies.

"What should we do?" Vance said.

I pointed up the slope—I could see a rock outcropping a klick or so away. "We climb," I said.

I pulled out my radio and called HQ. Berger was there, waiting for my call. I reported the situation.

"Yeah, we got that from the pilot," he said. "We've got a mother of a storm coming through in about an hour. You hole up in the radio shack."

"Trying to bury your mistake? I already told you the shack is going to end up in the river."

"You have your orders, soldier." I could hear him switch away from our frequency.

Not again, I thought. "They won't be able to evac us until this storm passes."

Athena looked at the desolation surrounding us. "Then we'll have to take care of ourselves."

I took heart from her false bravado.

"Can you walk?" she asked, turning up the collar of her jacket against the rain.

"You kidding?" I said. "My ankle's state of the art."

We started up the slope. Walking on the rough, moss-covered rocks was like walking on marbles. Every time my foot slipped, my ankle twisted, sending needles of pain up my leg. Athena tried to prop me up, but the weight and height difference made it impossible.

Still we stumbled on, ten meters, twenty, fifty, with one or the other of us falling flat every couple of minutes. By now, we were soaked to the bone and the temperature continued to drop, nearing freezing as indicated by the sleet now mixed in with the rain.

"I bet you wish you'd chosen augments," she said, putting her arm around my waist.

Before I could reply, the earth shook violently. We turned in time to see the radio shack slowly tilt, further, further, until it broke in half before sliding down the hill toward the water. The cliff now began another 500 meters farther up the hill.

"Come on!" I said to Vance, doubling my effort to climb.

Another hour of nightmare followed, slipping, gashing our knees on the rock, keeping our faces turned away from the thrashing rain. Twice more we felt the ground shake. Left alone, I might have given up and let the cold take me. I'd done it before. Athena wouldn't let me. Despite being wracked with shivers, she kept pushing me forward, each time saying, "God damn it, not here."

Finally I asked, "What do you mean, not here?"

"I mean, we're not going to die here. Not here."

I didn't reply; I'd told Saul the same thing an hour before he died.

We finally reached the rock outcropping. Old sandstone, like a headstone about as tall as I was and wide as my shoulder, with a hollow on the downwind side that could hold a large dog. The rain was relentless and the sun, faint behind the burdened clouds, was touching the horizon. It was the only shelter in sight.

I pushed Athena into the hollow space. "Draw up your legs," I said. "Form yourself into a ball."

"But there's not enough room for us both here," she said as she sat, pulled her knees to her chest, and encircled them with her arms. Her teeth chattered uncontrollably.

"That's OK," I said. "I'm going to be your blanket."

I knelt and leaned into her, pressing my chest to her face and chest, wrapping my arms around the rock that contained her, until my torso formed a shield for her against the rain and wind. My hands, exposed to the elements, immediately began to ache.

When she realized what I was doing, she started poking me in the ribs. "Stop it," she said. "God damn, I made those hands. You can't waste them like this."

"You did it once," I said. "You can do it again."

The cold was like a knife as I hugged that rock. I'd been through it once before and prayed that the numbness would come soon. I knew what I was going to lose, but I was determined to stay alive. For Athena. For Saul.

My head was nestled next to hers, her mouth by my ear.

I could tell she was crying as she said, over and over, "Good as new, Quinn. I promise. I'll make you good as new."

Funny thing was, with her in my arms, I felt good as new already, no matter what was to come.

Nevermind the Bollocks

By Annie Bellet

There were six different corridors that'd take a man up to the starship loading bays—and the bloody Jaysus knew how many rooms, halls, and other passageways leading into the six—and yet it seemed that whenever Diarmuid absolutely had to be at the docks *right freakin' now*, every bastard he owed something to or that wanted something from him managed to find their way into the particular path he'd chosen that time.

"Mick!" Big Rizzo, who was of course shorter than Diarmuid himself, stepped out of what Diarmuid imagined was a janitor's closet along with Little Rizzo and blocked the narrow corridor so he'd have to either run into them or stop dead.

"Bosses've called me up—can we have a chat later?" He tried to slide between them, but was hindered by a meaty arm.

"You promised you'd see about that licorice," Big Rizzo said.

"And the coffee, the real shit, not that imitation stuff that tastes like rocket fuel," Little Rizzo chimed in. His breath smelled a bit like rocket fuel, and Diarmuid started to despair of ever getting away from these gobshites.

"Fellows," he said, backing off a step and spreading his hands. Smiling hurt his pride, but getting his arse kicked wouldn't speed up his progress any. "This very shipment I'm hurrying to check on should have everything you require."

"We's paid you a cycle ago."

"That you did." He patted his breast pocket where his little book of wants and needs, checks and balances, rested. "We're buried under a moon in the middle of Jaysus knows. These things take time. I'm going right up to the shipment, and I'll have both you gentlemen satisfied soon. Don't worry, I'll find you."

"Don't you worry—we'll find you." Little Rizzo punctuated his speech with sharp finger jabs to Diarmuid's chest that would likely leave finger-sized bruises.

"See you," Big Rizzo said as they stepped aside just enough for Diarmuid to squeeze between them like sausage going through a grinder.

He waited until he couldn't hear their heavy breathing and heavier footfalls before he muttered, "Not if I see you first."

One turn and only scant seconds later, he heard a door skim open and a happy voice called out, "Hey! Mick!"

"Oh fook this," he said, and took off at a run.

"Yer late, Mick." Scorzani, the Boss's right-hand man, shook his head as Diarmuid stumbled into the control room overlooking the second and larger of the two docking bays.

"Sorry," Diarmuid said, mentally adding *Captain Obvious* as he resisted rolling his eyes heavenward. "So, you've got a weight problem?"

"Scuzzi?"

"The ship—that beauty in there. The weights were off from her cargo list?" Jaysus but he was crapping on all cylinders today.

"That's what the moron Carlito reported, but the crew checks out and they says they got nothing to do with anything, of course." Scorzani shrugged bull-like shoulders.

Diarmuid started checking the data. His little 'extras' like coffee and licorice and the silk panties for Donovan's sextomatons were all there and listed, their weights accounted for in the ship manifests. Each ship coming into the Arcadia system had to register cargo, crew, and exact weight minus the expected fuel burn for the incoming journey before one of the two techs, Diarmuid being one, would program in the coordinates.

The idiot Carlito wasn't wrong, though: this ship's weight was off by twenty-one point three six kilos.

"Scanned it for bugs, I assume?" he asked.

Scorzani pinched the bridge of his nose as though he had a headache and nodded. "Find the stinking issue. The ambrosia shipment's all processed and ready to go. Boss wants this done and off."

"Done and done, boss." Diarmuid rubbed sweating palms onto his trousers and let out a slow breath. What weighed twenty-one bloody kilos? A middling-size dog? Maybe one of the crew went on one hell of a diet?

"Good, Mick. I'm putting you in charge of this and I'll be reporting that straight to the Boss." Scorzani clapped him on the shoulder hard enough to knock him into the console, probably adding another bruise.

That's how it was here in Purgatory, as the lower echelons on the ambrosia processing station liked to call it. If there was a buck to be passed, it got passed quicker than kissing disease. Diarmuid squeezed his sweating hands into fists and tried to shove away the feeling that, once again, the music had stopped, and he'd been left standing in the spotlight with his trou bunched round his ankles. There was nothing for it but to get to work and come up with some kind of explanation that didn't get him retired as a shooting star in Arcadia's atmosphere.

Asteroids. That would be what he'd tell the bosses, Diarmuid decided after inspecting the bloody ship, digging through the manifests, and then jumping right into the meat of the onboard computer's code. Fooking asteroids.

The ship was one of the long, oblong star-runners and a real beauty—sleek and silvery, with excellent dynamics and engine to weight ratios—except for the hell of a dent some idiot had failed to notice in the aft hull. The records showed them stopping in the Beehive Cluster at one of the Family's twenty-two ansible arrays and then taking what they recorded as "minor" damage from an unforeseen asteroid shower around the planet they'd decided to orbit.

Bits of heavy iron and nickel-infused space rock had welded itself right into the hull underneath the bulbous lower cargo bays, where any bloke who wasn't blind with his hands missing could have found it on a routine inspection once the bloody thing got into dock. Not that it accounted for all twenty-one point three six kilos, though—Diarmuid had no fooking clue how the rest of that weight got in there, but his back was killing him and he still had multiple little "gifts" and sundries to deliver. This buck could now be safely jettisoned into space.

He compiled a report and forwarded it on up to Scorzani. Job complete. Except …

There were a few bits of junk code: little remnants that sometimes were stored where they shouldn't be so that when the main data was deleted, sections lived on … much like finding some broad's hair in your bed or perfume lingering on your pillow long after she'd taken all your money and run off with a man whose name people could actually pronounce.

Diarmuid popped his right shoulder and stared at the screen. The crew. This data seemed to say that something had changed with the crew, but the rest had been scrubbed out by a program that knew what it was up to. He brought up the manifest again. Six of the blokes he recognized from prior runs out to pick up shipments. Two others checked out with cross data from the last back-up they had of the general Family databases.

But the new sucker—a big, blocky-looking fellow who was supposedly a new station doctor, going by the name of Moretti. Diarmuid stared at the video replay of Dr. Moretti offloading from the ship and shook his head. If that man was a doctor, he'd slap a bonnet on himself and let the boys call him Mary Mags.

To top that off, the file was stamped "voluntary". If this bastard was a doctor, he was an idiot one. No one but the top few, those connected by blood, came "voluntary" to Purgatory.

Diarmuid sighed and punched the off button on the screen. He had people to see and places to avoid. Flagging this poor rat and then going through the mess of a DNA test and other nonsense would be a pain up the arse. With his luck lately, the bloke would be legit—and then he'd have another scary-fooking bloke looking for payback on his arse.

'Sides, if Diarmuid's luck were really turning for the besty, that nineteen-odd kilos he couldn't account for even with the asteroids would turn out to be a cleverly hidden bomb, and Dr. Moretti would blow this rock wide open.

"Legging it from the worst, hoping for the best," Diarmuid said to himself, and he whistled the whole way back down to his quarters.

He'd just pulled on his favorite paisley smoking jacket and poured a tumbler of neat scotch—the real stuff, peaty taste and everything—when his door chimed and the friendly computer voice (choice number five on the standard list) informed him that a guest was waiting in the foyer.

"The foyer" was an overly grand name for the space between the corridor door and the inner entrance, but Diarmuid tried to cling to what semblance of normalcy he could and he'd programmed the computer to refer to such things by their proper names. The damn program still called him Mick, though.

He flipped to the camera and saw LC-920 impatiently staring up into the viewer with her big doe eyes. Curious shite, this. The sextomatons never came to see him directly. Diarmuid was indentured. Sure, he was supposedly the top technician, but fooked if the sexbots cared about that. Probably figured he'd reprogram them to do something kinky. LC-920, or Elsie as she demanded to be called, was the only one who gave him the time, much less a spot of conversation. She was also the only one with a truly unique personality.

"Evening, Elsie." Diarmuid mustered up a smile as she sashayed into his one-room apartment. Apartment? Compartment, more like.

"You're awful brooksy for a canceled stamp, Mick," she said, leaning in to kiss him on the cheek before dancing by and hopping up onto the kitchenette counter. The beaded fringe on her dress shivered and tinkled as she moved.

Diarmuid had no clue what she'd just said ... but her blood-red lips were smiling, so he assumed it was something nice and inclined his head politely. Some history buff, and there were a surprising number of those in the Family, had decided that programming this particular bot with an archaic vocabulary would make for good craic. The bastard was half-right. Elsie had a bucketful of personality, but no one ever understood half of what spilled out from between her lips.

Diarmuid started, politely, to ask her what she wanted, but she brought a manicured finger to her mouth and then reached into her ample cleavage and drew out a small black box with a switch on it. She flipped it, and a chill crept up Diarmuid's spine as the room filled with almost imperceptible static.

A jammer. Shite.

He wracked his brain for what he might have said or done in his last encounter with her. Elsie appeared weak and harmless, but she took insults very personally and many a poor square had ended up accidently going down a maintenance shaft face first. Rule one of living on Purgatory: never underestimate Elsie.

"Come'ere, Mickie," she purred, crooking a finger at him.

He went with the reluctance of a moth mistaking a heat lamp for the moon, wondering if he was about to experience first-hand one of Elsie's "accidents".

"You're a flukey embalmer, Mick, but word is you always get things done." Her fingers trailed down and loosed the sash of his jacket, slipping inside to tangle in the light dusting of copper hairs on his lower belly.

He swallowed hard and tried to parse what she'd said. "You need something?" he asked. It was, after all, what his unofficial job had become, so it seemed a safe-ish guess.

"I do, Mick, I really do." Her hand slid down and undid his belt, then dived deeper. Sweat started trickling in an itchy line behind his ears and into his collar. "I want," she said, leaning forward so her lips were right beside his ear, "to get off this fucking rock."

Shite on a stick. His granpappy, Jaysus rest him, had taught Diarmuid to never argue with or refuse a woman whose hand was wrapped around his balls. He wasn't sure the old man had meant that literally, but seeing as Elsie's hand was currently stroking him somewhere around his 'barse, he really didn't want to have to tell her no.

And yet, she'd asked him for the one thing he probably couldn't procure: a way out of hell.

He pulled gently on her wrist, mentally kicking himself. Hopefully she'd kill him quickly and not leave him to spend the rest of his days drooling in a chair, handing out napkins in the men's room at Donovan's like the last sad sack who'd pissed her off.

"I can't do that, Elsie. I'm sorry, my lovely, but if I could get anyone off this rock, I'd go myself."

Her eyes narrowed, and Diarmuid started trying to remember

the words for the Last Rites. "But you'll escape. The sod busters get you eventually. I don't die. I just go right on petting these potatoes and rug hoppers until some wurp flips my switch or re-stitches me. I gotta scram before then, Mickie—I just have to."

He stood still, holding onto her hand, feeling the steel beneath the soft, fake skin and suddenly an image of the stone-faced doctor invaded his mind. The probable phony. He couldn't be in Purgatory without a reason, and if he were an infiltrator from a competitor … well, he'd have an escape plan, now, wouldn't he? Facing off against an unknown, cold-eyed bastard suddenly looked a lot better than trying to tell Elsie no again.

His heart thudding a million light-years a second, Diarmuid licked his lip and decided he wanted to live a little longer.

"All right, love," he said, bringing her fingers to his mouth in a gentle kiss that had his neglected balls lodging complaints. "Lend me that jammer there, and I'll see what I can do."

"No." She smiled. "I'm going along."

Diarmuid found himself shifting nervously from foot to foot inside the doctor's foyer, staring up into the camera. Elsie stood silent and vacuous beside him. She'd sworn on pain of reprogramming that she'd let him do all the talking.

"I'm Diarmuid O'Malley, chief tech. I need to come in and calibrate your monitor." Bloody lame excuse, but it worked most of the time on the non-techs. He wasn't sure how to explain Elsie, so he just left her out. Keeping things simple was usually the best plan—if there even was a plan.

There was silence for long enough that he started to wonder if the bloke would just ignore them. The station computer that Diarmuid had hacked into said that Moretti was inside his quarters, but that didn't mean he'd answer his door—especially if he happened to be some sort of foreign agent.

He didn't realized how much tension he'd been holding in until the inner doors slide apart and his legs turned to deck rubber. Cautiously, Diarmuid stepped inside an apartment that was nearly identical to his own, except for missing any and all personal features.

"Monitor works fine," Moretti said. He'd been so still that Diarmuid hadn't immediately seen him, and he gave a little start as the big man peeled away from the wall near the kitchenette.

Afraid he'd lose his nerve and leg it before getting what needed saying said, Diarmuid pulled out the jammer, strode over to the counter, and turned the thing on. Elsie's dress shimmered around her as she followed him.

"We come in peace," Elsie said with a wink after giving Moretti the once-over.

Diarmuid squeezed her arm and glared, trying to remind her with his eyes that she'd promised to shut her gob.

Moretti cracked his knuckles and tipped his head to one side, one pale eyebrow raised and his smoke-grey eyes as hard and friendly as ice cubes. At least his hands looked large enough to crack Diarmuid's neck in one quick blow—if this whole thing went arseways, his death might be even quicker than what grand old Elsie could deliver. If he really bollixed this up, maybe they'd both have a go together.

"Hear us out before you start cracking anything else," Diarmuid began, shuffling so that the counter was between him and the giant. "I know you aren't Moretti. If you're really a doctor, I'll … well, 'tisn't important what I'd do. My guess is you are the first honest-to-Jaysus infiltrator one of the others has managed to get into this rock. And hat's off to you, mate. Truly. Bold job. I'd guess Siberian Syndicate, eh?" A muscle twitched in the man's jaw, but he said nothing. "Not going to tell me? That's fine, that's right fine. But see, if I were a betting man—and I used to be, that and the light-skirts got me here—I'd bet that you are after the location of this place."

When he stopped to suck in a breath, the Siberian spoke, glancing back and forth between the two of them.

"You know what location of Ambrosia planet is worth?"

"Well, yes, mate. I do. And there are only five people inside this whole rock who know where it is. That's why ships have to stop at the arrays, so we can program the location into the drives and then scrub them when they get here, and why we make everyone jump away blind and undergo another scrub at the next array." Diarmuid licked his lips. The Siberian had folded his arms and was listening, leaning slightly forward, his eyes calculating instead of frozen. Time for the pitch.

"I'm one of the five. The location codes are in my head. Literally. And I'll give them to whomever you work for—on the condition that I and my friend blow off this rock, and are set with enough to see out our days somewhere comfortable and far fooking away from any Family."

"Tell me." The Siberian bared his teeth, even and white and almost sharp-looking, like a predator's.

"Not born yesterday, mate. Get us outta here first. You've got an escape plan, I assume?"

The Siberian laughed, the sound as heavy and grating as ungreased ball bearings rubbing together. "I show you plan." He opened his mouth and leaned in close enough that Diarmuid could almost taste the man's dinner, onion and protein compote. At the back of his mouth one of his molars was discolored, incongruous with the perfect teeth around it.

"Is cyanide. In my ear is recorder. Scans not find it because it is not activated until I give code word. I die when I have enough information and body goes out airlock. After body temperature drop to freezing or if hit atmosphere and burn, signal goes out and my people come."

"Cor, what a wurp," Elsie muttered from behind Diarmuid.

"Fooking Jaysus. That's cold." Diarmuid shook his head and slumped against the counter. The Siberian had likely planned to find out who had the code and then torture it out of them, killing himself afterward. Standard protocol was to jettison all bodies. Many ended up as corpsicles orbiting Purgatory; the rest were probably sucked down into Arcadia's atmosphere to become another flash over the ocean planet.

"If you want asylum, I can offer. But I cannot get us off this place. Maybe you have weapon? We could take that ship."

"No, no weapons on Purgatory. Not that it would matter. There's only two launch keys, and I mean physical keys that have to be turned for the doors to open and the launch magnets to activate. Those I don't have access to."

"Boxswiller. There's a gun on the station. And it's in the same spot as a key." Elsie danced in a little circle, half-singing the words.

"What?" Diarmuid turned to her and then realized what she meant. "Ah. That pea-shooter above the Boss's desk? That thing's a relic. Does it even have ammunition?"

"It shoots vegetables?" The Siberian looked lost.

"No, potato, it shoots people. With lead or something." Elsie gave him her most wicked grin, and Diarmuid knew the man truly was made of ice and stone when he didn't even blink, much less blush.

"Can you get the key and the gun, Elsie?"

"I can fix it. Boss is a real cuddler who likes to take too much lap in that back room at Donovan's nosebaggery. I get him drowned enough, I can take whatever I want." She chewed the inside of her cheek, thinking. "You beggars will have to be ready, though, with our ride. My hijinks won't go skulky forever."

"Translation?" The Siberian looked at Diarmuid.

"She's going to get the Boss drunk and take the key and the gun, and we'd better be ready to scram on the ship whenever she shows up," Diarmuid said in a rush before Elsie could take offense at the Siberian not understanding her. It was her main peeve.

"Good. Let us make plan." The Siberian smiled, and Diarmuid almost started to believe that they'd really be able to do this.

The adrenaline high of charging into certain doom thinking they could win had worn a bit threadbare by the wee hours of the next morning. Diarmuid stood in the console room of docking bay two, programming the cameras onto quick video loops as he tried not to think about the sounds of struggling and choking coming from behind him. The Siberian had the poor sod who'd drawn night duty in a headlock and was slowly squeezing the life right out of him.

"Eh, don't kill him, all right? Just stuff him in that closet when he stops kicking. We'll be out before he wakes up," Diarmuid called over his shoulder.

"You let me kill the others," the Siberian said, with just a hint of a whine in his flat voice.

"Aye, well, those arse-monkeys deserved that. Rossi here is just a kid. Let 'im be." Diarmuid smiled grimly, and started downloading the flight instructions and codes into his hand-held so he could start the ship from the ground whenever Elsie showed up with the key. If she showed up at all.

He and the Siberian had run into a spot of trouble on the way up to the dock, but the big, quiet man had dispatched Little Rizzo and Big Rizzo before Diarmuid could so much as squeak, much less flee. He'd secretly taken a little sadistic pleasure in helping the Siberian haul their bodies into a side closet, the two bastards' necks at odd angles and only a blissfully silent trickle of blood dripping out of each normally unstoppable mouth.

Cameras reprogrammed and codes entered, Diarmuid turned and motioned for the Siberian to follow him down the steep metal steps to the launch bay.

Crate upon crate of ambrosia, the drug harvested from the planet's oceans, stood stacked three men high, waiting on the dock workers to load them into the gaping belly of the ship. Bloody ambrosia. It was what sustained the entire Family enterprise—a drug more powerful than any of the old world variety. Bliss in a tiny candy package. Diarmuid almost wished the ship had already been loaded, though it would have been tougher to steal at that point. A shipment of this size would be worth a fooking lot.

The door just behind them at the base of the long bay slid open and the Siberian yanked him behind a crate. It was only Elsie, however, and Diarmuid rubbed his arm once the giant let him go. That would likely bruise as well.

Before he had a chance to say a word to Elsie—who was grinning like a cat about to drown in a milk carrier—another door, this one over on the loading side of the bay, opened and six of the workers sauntered in, laughing and jeering. They had their hard-hats and gloves on, clearly about to begin loading up the shipment.

"Jaysus," he muttered as Elsie ducked down behind the crates with them. "Key?"

"Here," she said, handing it over. "Boss won't be petting much nor needing that."

"We go then? What about them?" The Siberian popped his head around the crate and looked at the men clustered by the far door.

"See that panel?" Diarmuid whispered, pointing across to where a big control panel was built into the wall. "This key goes into that flashing red slot there." In plain bloody view of all those bastards, naturally.

Could the Siberian and Elsie get over there and take all those guys out? Maybe. Before one of them ducked through the door and hit the alarm? Likely not. The game was up.

"Put your teeth back out, Mickie." Elsie chucked him under the chin hard enough that said teeth rattled against each other. "I can take care of those potatoes. You get the key in and boost our ride. Goofy here can stump his stilts and get on the ship. Berries?"

"She said to—" Diarmuid started to translate.

"Clear. I get to ship, she takes care of them, you insert key."

Diarmuid swallowed, and wished he'd taken a longer piss before leaving his room for the final time that night.

"Elsie, ah, how will you—" he whispered to her, but she touched his lips and shook her head.

Standing up, she pulled off her dress, revealing a bouncy pair of anti-gravitational breasts and a large six-shooter gun. The relic. Diarmuid had heard that this was the pistol that shot some Family bloke named Hoffa centuries earlier. Elsie winked at him and tucked the gun behind her back.

"Those potatoes got no eyes," she said, and then she stepped out from behind the crates.

Diarmuid waited until he heard the men whistling and calling out to her, and then he made like a rabbit and bolted for the panel. From the side he heard Elsie say, "Sorry, boys—this bank is closed."

Six loud pops echoed around the bay, each followed by a scream and a thud. One poor sot kept on screaming. Diarmuid gritted his teeth and fumbled the key up into the slot, punching in codes on his hand-held. Heat and friction started dancing off the ship as the engines powered up and the magnets began to shift together.

"Go!" he yelled to Elsie.

They bolted for the ship nearly side by side and the Siberian helped pull them up into the quickly closing lift. Giving commands through his hand-held, Diarmuid raced up the central corridor toward the pilot's bridge.

The ship sealed and pressurized, and the artificial gravity pressed in on them just in time for the magnets to engage fully and start sliding them out toward the far doors. The key had done its trick, and the thick metal was sliding open as they gained speed and barreled toward it.

Diarmuid strapped into the pilot seat and allowed himself a whoop. A dead body smashed down over the viewport as the docking bay depressurized and its contents were sucked out. Globs of the bastard's blood sped ahead of them like parade balloons.

"Not a good death," the Siberian commented as he dropped down into the co-pilot's chair.

"They broke the first rule of Purgatory," Diarmuid said, entering coordinates for the Beehive system into the nav computer.

"What is?"

Diarmuid smiled as Elsie, still naked, slid into the Siberian's lap and planted a kiss on his cheek.

"Don't ever underestimate Elsie," said Diarmuid.

This time, the Siberian blushed. The engines engaged, and the ship torpedoed like one of Elsie's pea-shooter bullets out into the vastness of space. For a moment, the vast water world of Arcadia appeared on the screen, and then the blue and white marble was gone behind them.

"Leaving Hell," Diarmuid said, leaning back after punching the shielding down on the viewport. "Next stop: anywhere fooking else."

CPSIA information can be obtained at www.ICGtesting.com
Printed in the USA
VOW110717080212

7668LV00002B/105/P